PUFFIN BOOKS

Editor: Kaye Webb

MY NAUGHTY LITTLE SISTER

These stories, originally told on the B.B.C.'s programme *Listen with Mother*, have become established favourites for reading aloud. They are a mother's own stories, told to her own children, about the little sister of her own childhood.

Every mother is familiar with the plea 'Tell me about when *you* were naughty' and the device of a little sister who gets into trouble is a brilliantly diplomatic solution.

These enchanting stories describe all the ordinary small events of a child's daily life and the pitfalls into which the adventurous can tumble.

They are told with gaiety and imagination and at just the right pace for small children of between three and six.

EMiLy 3y

My Naughty Little

PENGUIN BOOKS

Sister

DOROTHY EDWARDS

Illustrated by Henrietta Garland

Penguin Books Ltd, Harmondsworth, Middlesex, England
Penguin Books Australia Ltd, Ringwood, Victoria, Australia

—

First published by Methuen 1952
Published in Puffin Books 1959
Reprinted with three additional stories
(from *More Naughty Little Sister Stories*) 1963
Reprinted 1964, 1965, 1967, 1969, 1970

—

Copyright © Dorothy Edwards, 1952

—

Made and printed in Great Britain
by Richard Clay (The Chaucer Press) Ltd, Bungay, Suffolk
Set in Monotype Garamond

FOR MY SISTER
PHIL

By the same author
My Naughty Little Sister's Friends

Contents

I

The Very First Story

A VERY long time ago, when I was a little girl, I didn't have a naughty little sister at all. I was a child *all on my own*. I had a father and a mother of course, but I hadn't any other little brothers or sisters – I was *quite alone*.

I was a very lucky little girl because I had a dear grannie and a dear grandad and lots of kind aunts and uncles to make a fuss of me. They played games with me, and gave me toys and took me for walks, and bought me ice-creams and told me stories, but I *hadn't* got a little sister.

Well now, one day, when I was a child on my own, I went to stay with my kind godmother-aunt in the country. My kind godmother-aunt was very good to me. She took me out every day to see the farm animals and to pick flowers, and she read stories to me, and let me cook little cakes and jam tarts in her oven, and I was very, very happy. I didn't want to go home one bit.

Then, one day, my godmother-aunt said, 'Here is a letter from your father, and *what* do you think he says?'

My aunt was smiling and smiling. 'What do you think he says?' she asked. 'He says that you have a little baby sister waiting for you at home!'

I *was* excited! I said, 'I think I had better go home AT ONCE, don't you?' and my kind godmother-aunt said, 'I think you had indeed.' And she took me home that very day!

My aunt took me on a train and a bus and another bus, and then I was home!

And, do you know, before I'd even got indoors, I heard a waily-waily noise coming from the house, and my godmother-aunt said, 'That is your new sister.'

'Waah-waah,' my little sister was saying, 'waah-waah.'

I was surprised to think that such a very new child could make so much noise, and I ran straight indoors and straight upstairs and straight into my mother's bedroom. And there was my good kind mother sitting up in bed smiling and smiling, and there, in a cot that used to be my old cot, was my new cross little sister crying and crying!

My mother said, 'Sh-sh, baby, here is your big sister come to see you.' My mother lifted my naughty little baby sister out of the cot, and my little sister stopped crying at once.

My mother said, 'Come and look.'

My little sister was wrapped up in a big woolly white shawl, and my mother undid the shawl and there was my little sister! When my mother put her down on the bed, my little sister began to CRY AGAIN.

She was a little, little red baby, crying and crying. 'Waah-waah, waah-waah,' – like that. Isn't it a nasty noise?

My little sister had tiny hands and tiny little feet. She went on crying and crying, and curling up her toes, and beating with her arms in a very cross way.

My mother said, 'She likes being lifted up and cuddled. She is a very good baby when she is being cuddled and fussed, but when I put her down she cries and cries. She is an *artful pussy*,' my mother said.

I was very sorry to see my little sister crying, and I was disappointed because I didn't want a crying little sister very much, but I went and looked at her. I looked at her little red face and her little screwed up eyes and her little crying mouth and then I said, 'Don't cry baby, don't cry baby.'

And, do you know, when I said, 'Don't cry baby,' my little sister *stopped crying*, really stopped crying at once. For me! Because *I* told her to. She opened her eyes and she looked and looked and she didn't cry any more.

My mother said, 'Just fancy! She must know you are her own big sister! She has stopped crying.'

I was pleased to think that my little sister had stopped crying because she knew I was her big sister, and I put my finger on my sister's tiny, tiny hand and my little sister caught hold of my finger tight with her little curly fingers.

My mother said I could hold my little sister on my lap if I was careful. So I sat down on a chair and my godmother-aunt put my little sister on to my lap, and I held her very carefully; and my little sister didn't cry at all. She went to sleep like a good baby.

And do you know, she was so small and so sweet and she held my finger so tightly with her curly little fingers that I loved her and loved her and although she often cried after that I never minded it a bit, because I knew how nice and cuddly she could be when she was good!

2

Going Fishing

A LONG time ago when I was a little girl, I had a sister who was littler than me. My little sister had brown eyes, and red hair, and a pinkish nose, and she was very, very stubborn.

When you told her to smile for her photograph, she said, 'No, I don't want to,' but if you gave her an ice-cream, or a chocolate biscuit, or a toffee-drop, she said 'Thank you,' and smiled and smiled.

So you must try to imagine her with a chocolate biscuit *and* an ice-cream *and* a toffee-drop, so that you can see her at her very, very best. . . .

Imagine very hard. . . . There, doesn't she look a bright, happy child?

Well now, I'm going to tell you some stories about her which I think you will like.

The first story is called GOING FISHING, and here it is:

One day, when I was a little girl, and my sister was a very little girl, some children came to our house and asked my mother if I could go fishing with them.

They had jam-jars with string on them, and fishing-nets, and sandwiches, and lemonade.

My mother said 'Yes' – I could go with them; and she found *me* a jam-jar and a fishing-net, and cut *me* some sandwiches.

Then my naughty little sister said, 'I want to go! I want to go!' Just like that. So my mother said I might as well take her too.

Then my mother cut some sandwiches for my little sister, but she didn't give her a jam-jar or a fishing-net because she said she was too little to go near the water. My mother gave my little sister a basket to put stones in, because my little sister liked to pick up stones, and she gave me a big bottle of lemonade to carry for both of us.

My mother said, 'You mustn't let your little sister get herself wet. You must keep her away from the water.' And I said, 'All right, Mother, I promise.'

So then we went off to the little river, and we took our shoes off and our socks off, and tucked up our clothes, and we went into the water to catch fish with our fishing-nets, and we filled our jam-jars with water to put the fishes in when we caught them. And we said to my naughty little sister, 'You mustn't come, you'll get yourself wet.'

Well, we paddled and paddled and fished and fished, but we didn't catch any fish at all, not one little tiny one even. Then a boy said, 'Look, there is your little sister in the water too!'

And, do you know, my naughty little sister had walked right into the water with her shoes and socks on, and she was trying to fish with her little basket.

I said, 'Get out of the water,' and she said, 'No.'

I said, 'Get out *at once*,' and she said, 'I don't want to.'

I said, 'You'll get all wet,' and she said, 'I don't care.' Wasn't she naughty?

So I said, 'I must fetch you out then,' and my naughty little sister tried to run away in the water. Which is a silly thing to do because she fell down and got all wet.

She got her frock wet, and her petticoat wet, and her knickers wet, and her vest wet, and her hair wet, and her hair-ribbon – all soaking wet. Of course, I told you her shoes and socks were wet before.

And she cried and cried.

So we fetched her out of the water, and we said,

'Oh, dear, she will catch a cold,' and we took off her
wet hat, and her wet frock, and her wet petticoat,
and her wet knickers, and her wet vest, and her wet
hair-ribbon, *and* her wet shoes and socks, and we
hung all the things to dry on the bushes in the sunshine, and we wrapped my naughty little sister up
in a woolly cardigan.

My little sister *cried and cried*.

So we gave her the sandwiches, and she ate them
all up. She ate up her sandwiches and my sandwiches, and the other children's sandwiches all up –
and she cried and cried.

Then we gave her the lemonade and she spilled it
all over the grass, and she cried and cried.

Then one of the children gave her an apple, and
another of the children gave her some toffees, and,
while she was eating these, we took her clothes off
the bushes and ran about with them in the sunshine
until they were dry. When her clothes were quite
dry, we put them all back on her again, and she
screamed and screamed because she didn't want her
clothes on any more.

So, I took her home, and my mother said, 'Oh,
you've let your little sister fall into the water.'

And I said, 'How do you know? Because we dried
all her clothes,' and my mother said, 'Ah, but you
didn't *iron* them.' My little sister's clothes were all
crumpled and messy.

Then my mother said I should not have any sugary biscuits for supper because I was disobedient. Only bread and butter, and she said my little sister must go straight to bed, and have some hot milk to drink.

And my mother said to my little sister, 'Don't you think you were a naughty little girl to go in the water?'

And my naughty little sister said, 'I won't do it any more, because it was too wet.'

But, do you know, when my mother went to throw away the stones out of my little sister's basket, she found a little fish in the bottom which my naughty little sister had caught!

3

My Naughty Little Sister
at the Fair

HERE is another story about my naughty little sister:

When I was a little girl, my little sister used to eat all her breakfast up, and all her dinner up, and all her tea up, and all her supper up – every bit.

But one day my naughty little sister wouldn't eat her breakfast. She had cornflakes and an egg, and a piece of bread and butter, and an apple, and a big cup of milk, and she wouldn't eat anything.

She said, 'No cornflakes.'

Then my mother said, 'Well, eat your egg, then,' and she said, 'No egg. Nasty egg.' She said 'Nasty apple,' too, and she spilled her milk all over the table. Wasn't she naughty?

My mother said, 'You won't go to the fair this afternoon if you don't eat it all up.' So then my naughty little sister began to eat up her breakfast very quickly, she ate the cornflakes and the egg, but she really couldn't manage the apple, and my mother said, 'Well, you ate most of your breakfast so I think we shall let you go to the fair.'

Shall I tell you why my naughty little sister hadn't wanted to eat her breakfast? *She was too excited*. And when my naughty little sister was excited, she was very cross and disobedient.

When the fair-time came, my big cousin Jane came to fetch us. Then my naughty little sister got so excited that she was crosser than ever. My mother dressed her up in her new best blue dress and her new best blue knickers, and her white shoes and blue socks, but my naughty little sister wouldn't help a bit. And you know what that means.

She went all stiff and stubborn, and she wouldn't put her arms in the arm-holes for herself, and she wouldn't lift up her feet for her shoes, and my mother said, 'Very well, they shall go without you.' Then my naughty little sister lifted up her feet very quickly. Wasn't she bad?

We went on a bus to the fair, and when we got there, it was very nice. We saw cows, and horses, and pigs, and sheep, and chickens, and lots and lots of people. And there were big swings that went swingy-swing, swingy-swing, and roundabouts that went round and round, round and round. Then my naughty little sister said, 'I want a swing! I want a swing!'

But my big cousin Jane said, 'No, you are too little for those big swings, but you shall go on the little roundabout.'

The little roundabout had wooden horses with real reins, and things to put your feet in, and there were little cars on the roundabout, and a little red fire-engine, and a little train.

First, we watched the roundabout going round and round, and when it went round all the cars and horses went up and down, up and down, and the fire-engine and the train went up and down too. The roundabout played music as it went round.

Then, when it stopped, my big cousin said, 'Get on, both of you.' There were lots of other children there, and some of them were afraid to go on the roundabout, but my little sister wasn't afraid. She was the first child to go on, and she got on all by herself, without *anyone* lifting her at all. Wasn't she a big girl? And do you know what she did? She got into the seat of the red fire-engine, and rang and rang the bell. 'Clonkle! Clonkle! Clonkle!' went the bell, and my little sister laughed and laughed, and when the roundabout went round it played nice music, and my naughty little sister said, 'Hurrah. I'm going to put the fire out!'

My little sister had four rides on the round-about. One, two, three, four rides. And then my big cousin Jane said, 'We have spent all our money. We will go and look at the people buying horses.'

But my little sister got thoroughly nasty again, and she said, 'No horse. Nasty horses. Want round-about.' There, wasn't that bad of her? I'm glad you're not like that.

But my cousin said, 'Come along at once,' and my naughty little sister had to come, but do you know what she did, while we were looking at the horses? *She ran away.* I said she was a naughty child, you know.

Yes. She ran away, and we couldn't find her any-where. We looked and looked. We went to the roundabouts and she wasn't there. We went to the swings and she wasn't there. She wasn't at the pig place, or the cow place, or the chicken place, or any of the other places. So then my big cousin Jane said, 'We must ask a policeman. Because policemen are good to lost children.'

We asked a lady if she could tell us where a policeman was, and the lady said, 'Go over the road to the police-station.'

So my cousin took me over the road to the police-station, and we went into a big doorway, and through another door, and we saw a policeman sitting without his hat on. And the policeman said, 'How do you do, children? Can I help you?' Wasn't that nice of him?

Then my big cousin Jane said, 'We have lost a naughty little girl.' And she told the nice policeman all about my bad little sister, all about what her name was, and where we had lost her, and what she looked like, and the nice policeman wrote it all down in a big book.

Then the kind policeman said, 'No, we haven't a little girl here, but if we find her, we will send her home to you in a big car.'

So then my cousin Jane and I went home, and it was a long long walk, because we had spent all our pennies on the roundabout.

When we got home, what do you think? There was my naughty little sister, sitting at the table, eating her tea. She had got home before us after all. And do you know why that was? It was because a kind policeman had found her and taken her home in his big car.

And do you know, my naughty little sister said

she'd never, never run off like that again, because it wasn't at all nice, being lost. She said it made her cry.

But, my naughty little sister said, if she did get lost again, she would find another nice policeman to take her home, because policemen are so kind to lost children.

4

When my Naughty Little Sister
wasn't Well

I HOPE you aren't a shy child. My naughty little
sister wasn't shy, but she used to pretend to be
sometimes, and when nice aunts and uncles came to
see us, she wouldn't say, 'How do you do!' or shake
hands or anything, and if they tried to talk to her she
would run off down the garden and hide among the
currant bushes until they went away.

But my naughty little sister talked and talked
when she wanted to. She talked to the milkman, and
the baker, and the coalman, and the window-cleaner
man, and all the other people who came to the door,
and when they came she got terribly in their way,
because she talked to them so much, but they all
liked my naughty little sister.

One day she upset all the milkman's bottles, and
he only said, 'Never mind, no use crying over spilt
milk,' and another day she shut the cellar up just as
the coalman was going to tip the coal in, and he
only said, 'Well, well now, there's a job for your
father!' and she climbed up the ladder after the
window-cleaning man and then she cried because she

was afraid to come down, but *he* only said, 'There! There! Don't cry, dearie,' and he lent her his leathery thing to wipe her tears on.

So you see, they liked my naughty little sister very much, but wasn't she naughty?

Well now, one day my poor naughty little sister wasn't very well. She sat in her chair and looked very miserable and said, 'I'm not a very well girl today.'

So my mother said, 'You shall go to bed and have a hot drink, and a hot-water bottle and we shall send for the doctor to come and see what's wrong with you.'

And my naughty little sister said, 'No doctor! Nasty doctor!' Wasn't she a silly cuckoo? Fancy saying 'No doctor' when she wasn't well!

But my mother said, 'He's a nice doctor. You must tell him how you feel, and then he will make you all better.'

Then my naughty little sister said, 'I'm too shy. I won't talk to him.' She said it in a cross, growly voice, 'I *won't* talk to him!'

So my naughty little sister went to bed, and she had a hot-water bottle and a hot drink. Also, she had her best books, and all her dolls and her teddy bears, but she felt so not-well that she didn't want any of these things at all.

Presently my naughty little sister heard a knock at

the front door, and she said, 'No doctor,' and hid her face under the sheet.

But it wasn't the doctor, it was the nice milkman, and when he heard my naughty little sister wasn't well, he sent her his love, and a note-book with lines on, and a blue pencil to write with.

Then my naughty little sister heard the front door again, and she said, 'No doctor,' again, and hid her face again, but it was the nice baker, and he sent my naughty little sister *his* love and a little spongy cake in case she fancied it.

Then she heard the front door again, and she said, 'No doctor – nasty doctor,' but it was the nice coal-man, and he sent my naughty little sister *his* love and a red rose from his cap that smelt rosy and coaly.

After that my naughty little sister began to feel a much happier girl, and she didn't hide her face any more, so that when the window-cleaner man came to clean the window, she could see him smiling through the glass, and when he popped his head in and asked, 'How's the invalid?' my naughty little sister said, 'I'm not a well girl today.'

The window-cleaner man said, 'Well, the doctor will soon put you right.'

And my naughty little sister watched the window-cleaner man rubbing away with the leathery thing, and then she said, 'No doctor,' to the window-cleaner man. 'No doctor,' she said, out loud.

'Yes, doctor,' said the window-cleaner man.

'No doctor,' said my naughty little sister.

'That's a silly idea you've got,' said the window-cleaner man. 'The doctor will make you a well girl again.'

Then my naughty little sister began to cry and cry. 'No doctor, no doctor, I'm too shy.' Like that, in that miserable way.

And then the window-cleaner man said, 'What a pity you won't have the doctor, because you won't see his listening-thing, or his glass-stick-thing to pop under your tongue, or the doctor's bag that he keeps his little bottles in.'

Then my naughty little sister stopped crying and said, 'What listening-thing? What stick-thing?'

'Ah,' said the window-cleaning man, 'I shan't tell you that. Why should I? But it's a pity you won't see that doctor and find out for yourself.' That's what the window-cleaner man said.

Then the window-cleaner man went away, and took his ladder with him, and my naughty little sister stayed in her bed and thought and thought.

And presently, when she heard a knock at the front door, my naughty little sister didn't say, 'No doctor,' and hide her face under the sheet, even though it really *was* the doctor this time. She didn't do anything silly like that at all.

My naughty little sister waited and waited until

she heard my mother coming upstairs with the doctor, and when the doctor came into her bedroom my naughty little sister didn't say, 'Go away,' or pretend to be shy, or scream, or do any of the bad things she could do.

She said, 'Hallo, doctor,' and then the doctor said, 'Hallo, and how are you today?' and my naughty little sister said, 'I'm not a well girl today.'

Then she said, 'Have you got your doctor's bag, and your listening-thing, and your glass-stick-thing to pop into my mouth?' and the doctor said, 'Yes, I have.'

Then my naughty little sister was pleased as pleased, and she liked the doctor so much after all, that she took all the medicine he sent her without being cross once, and got a well girl again very quickly.

5

My Naughty Little Sister makes a Bottle-Tree

ONE day, when I was a little girl, and my naughty little sister was a littler girl, my naughty little sister got up very early one morning, and while my mother was cooking the breakfast, my naughty little sister went quietly, quietly out of the kitchen door, and quietly, quietly up the garden-path. Do you know why she went *quietly* like that? It was because she was *up to mischief*.

She didn't stop to look at the flowers, or the marrows or the runner-beans, and she didn't put her fingers in the water-tub. No! She went right along to the tool-shed to find a trowel. You know what trowels are, of course, but my naughty little sister didn't. She called the trowel 'a digger'.

'Where is the digger?' said my naughty little sister to herself.

Well, she found the trowel, and she took it down the garden until she came to a very nice place in the big flower-bed. Then she stopped and began to dig and dig with the trowel, which you know was a most naughty thing to do, because of all the little baby seeds that are waiting to come up in flower-beds sometimes.

Shall I tell you why my naughty little sister dug that hole? All right, I will. It was because she wanted to plant a brown shiny acorn. So, when she had made a really nice deep hole, she put the acorn in it, and covered it all up again with earth, until the brown shiny acorn was all gone.

Then my naughty little sister got a stone, and a leaf, and a stick, and she put them on top of the hole, so that she could remember where the acorn was, and then she went indoors to have her hands washed for breakfast. She didn't tell me, or my mother or anyone about the acorn. She kept it for her secret.

Well now, my naughty little sister kept going down the garden all that day, to look at the stone, the leaf, and the stick, on top of her acorn-hole, and my naughty little sister smiled and smiled to herself because she knew that there was a brown shiny acorn under the earth.

But when my father came home, he was very cross. He said, 'Who's been digging in my flower-bed?'

And my little sister said, 'I have.'

Then my father said, 'You are a bad child. You've disturbed all the little baby seeds!'

And my naughty little sister said, 'I don't care

about the little baby seeds, I want a home for my brown shiny acorn.'

So my father said, 'Well, *I* care about the little baby seeds myself, so I shall dig your acorn up for you, and you must find another home for it,' and he dug it up for her at once, and my naughty little sister tried all over the garden to find a new place for her acorn.

But there were beans and marrows and potatoes and lettuce and tomatoes and roses and spinach and radishes, and no room at all for the acorn, so my naughty little sister grew crosser and crosser and when tea-time came she wouldn't eat her tea. Aren't you glad you don't show off like that?

Then my mother said, 'Now don't be miserable. Eat up your tea and you shall help me to plant your acorn in a bottleful of water.'

So my naughty little sister ate her tea after all, and then my mother, who was a clever woman, filled a bottle with water, and showed my naughty little sister how to put the acorn in the top of the bottle. Shall I tell you how she did it, in case you want to try?

Well now, my naughty little sister put the pointy end of the acorn into the water, and left the bottom of the acorn sticking out of the top – (the bottom end, you know, is the end that sits in the little cup when it's on the tree).

'Now,' said my mother, 'you can watch its little root grow in the water.'

My naughty little sister had to put her acorn in lots of bottles of water, because the bottles were always getting broken, as she put them in such funny places. She put them on the kitchen window-sill where the cat walked, and on the side of the bath, and inside the bookcase, until my mother said, 'We'll put it on top of the cupboard, and I will get it down for you to see every morning after breakfast.'

Then at last, the little root began to grow. It pushed down, down into the bottle of water and it made lots of other little roots that looked just like whitey fingers, and my little sister was pleased as pleased. Then, one day, a little shoot came out of the top of the acorn, and broke all the browny outside off, and on this little shoot were two little baby leaves, and the baby leaves grew and grew, and my mother said, 'That little shoot will be a big tree one day.'

My naughty little sister was very pleased. When she was pleased she danced and danced, so you can just guess how she danced to think of her acorn growing into a tree.

'Oh,' she said, 'when it's a tree we can put a swing on it, and I can swing indoors on my very own tree.'

But my mother said, 'Oh, no. I'm afraid it won't like being indoors very much now, it will want to grow out under the sky.'

Then my little sister had a good idea. And now, this is a *good thing* about my little sister – she had a *very kind thought* about her little tree. She said, 'I know! When we go for a walk we'll take my bottle-tree and the digger (which, of course, you call a trowel) and we will plant it in the park, just where there are no trees, so it can grow and grow and spread and spread into a big tree.'

And that is just what she did do. Carefully, carefully, she took her bottle-tree out of the bottle, and put it in her little basket, and then we all went out to the park. And when my little sister had found a good place for her little bottle-tree, she dug a nice deep hole for it, and then she put her tree into the hole, and gently, gently put the earth all round its roots, until only the leaves and stem were showing, and when she'd planted it in, my mother showed her how to pat the earth with the trowel.

Then at last the little tree was in the kind of place it really liked, and my little sister had planted it all by herself.

Now you will be pleased to hear that the little bottle-tree grew and grew and now it's quite a big tree. Taller than my naughty little sister, and she's quite a big lady nowadays.

6

The Wiggly Tooth

WHEN I was a little girl, and my naughty little sister was a very little girl, we used to have an apple-tree in our garden, and sometimes my naughty little sister used to pick the apples and eat them. It was a very easy thing to do because the branches were so low.

So, my mother told us we were not to pick the apples. My mother said, 'It is naughty to pick the apples when they are growing upon the tree, because we want them to go on growing until they are ripe and rosy, and then we shall pick them and put them quite away for the winter-time.

'If you want an apple,' my mother said, 'you must pick up a windfall and bring it to me, and I will wash it for you.'

As you know, 'windfalls' are apples that fall off the tree on to the grass, so, one day, my little sister looked under the tree and found a nice big windfall on the grass, and she took it in for my mother to wash.

When my mother had washed the apple, *and* cut out the specky bit where the little maggot had gone to live, my little sister sat down on the step to eat her big apple.

She opened her mouth very wide, because it *was* such a big apple, and she took a big bite. And what do you think happened? She felt a funny cracky sort of feeling in her mouth. My naughty little sister was so surprised that she nearly tumbled off the step when she felt the funny cracky feeling in her mouth, and she put in her finger to see what the crackiness was, and she found that one of her nice little teeth was loose.

So my naughty little sister ran indoors to my mother, and she said, 'Oh, dear, my tooth has gone all loose and wiggly, what shall I do?' in a waily whiny voice because at first she didn't like it very much.

My mother said, 'There's nothing to worry about. All your nice little baby-teeth will come out one by one to make room for your big grown-up teeth.'

'Have a look, have a look,' said my naughty little sister. So my mother had a look, and then she said, 'It's just as I thought, there is a new little tooth peeping through already.'

So after that my little sister had a loose tooth, and she used to wiggle it and wiggle it with her finger. She used to wiggle it so much that the tooth got looser and looser.

When the nice baker came, my naughty little

sister showed him the tooth, and she showed the milkman and the window-cleaner man, and sometimes she used to climb up to the mirror and wiggle it hard, to show herself, because she thought that a loose tooth was a very special thing to have.

After a while, my mother said, 'Your tooth is so very loose, you had better let me take it out for you.'

But my naughty little sister didn't want to lose her lovely tooth, because she liked wiggling it so much, and she wouldn't let my mother take it out at all.

Then my mother said, 'Well, pull it out yourself then,' and my silly little sister said, 'No, I like it like this.'

The next time the window-cleaner man came, he said, 'Isn't that toothy-peg out yet?'

And my naughty little sister said, 'No. It's still here.' And she opened her mouth very wide to show the window-cleaner man that it was still there.

The window-cleaner man said, 'Why don't you pull it out? It's hanging on a threddle, it is indeed.'

My naughty little sister told him that she liked to have it to wiggle and to show people.

So the window-cleaner man said, 'You'd better take it to show the dentist.'

My naughty little sister said why should she take it to the dentist? Because she hadn't heard much about dentists, and the window-cleaner man who knew all about doctors and dentists and about how the sun moves and how pumpkins grow, told my naughty little sister all about dentists, how they looked after people's teeth for them, and made teeth for grown-up people who hadn't any of their own.

The window-cleaner man told my naughty little sister that *his* teeth were dentist-teeth and they were much prettier than his old ones, and my naughty little sister was very interested, and she said she would like the dentist to see her wiggly tooth.

So, the next time my mother said, 'What about that tooth, now?' My naughty little sister said, 'I want to go to the dentist.'

My mother said, 'Goodness me, surely it's loose enough for you to pull out yourself now?'

But my naughty little sister started to cry, 'I want to go to the dentist. I want to go, I do.' In a miserable voice like that.

So my mother said, 'Very well then. I want the dentist to see your teeth anyway, so we shall go as soon as he can see you!'

Well now, the dentist was a very nice man, he said he thought he'd really better see my naughty little sister's tooth right away.

When my mother and my little sister arrived at the dentist's they had to wait in the waiting-room with a lot of other people. My naughty little sister told all these other people about her wiggly tooth, and she showed it to them, and they all said what a lucky child she was to have such a wiggly tooth.

When it was my naughty little sister's turn to see the dentist, she was very pleased. She sat on his big chair and let him have a good look.

The dentist said, 'It's a very nice tooth, old lady. I'm sorry you don't want it taken out.'

'I want it to wiggle with,' said my silly little sister. Then my little sister asked all about making teeth and everything, and the dentist told her very nicely.

'It's a pity you don't want to part with that tooth though,' he said, 'because I should just like a tooth like that for my collection. I collect really nice teeth,' the dentist said.

My naughty little sister thought and thought, and she couldn't help seeing how very nice it would be to have a tooth in a real collection, so, do you know what she did? She put her hand up to her mouth, as quick as quick, and then she said, 'Here you are,' and there, right in the middle of her hand was her little tooth. She'd pulled it out all her very self.

7

The Fairy-Doll

WHEN I was a little girl, I had a fairy-doll that was so beautiful that I never wanted to play with it.

It had real shiny wings, and a shiny crown, and a fairy-wand, and a sticking-out dress with golden stars on it, and it shut its eyes when you laid it down and opened them when you stood it up and said, 'ma-ma,' if you tipped it forwards.

It was so beautiful, that I kept it in its box, wrapped up in white paper, in the drawer of my mother's wardrobe. I used to go and peep at it whenever I specially wanted to.

Well now, my naughty little sister had a doll too. Her doll was a very poor old thing, with no eyes left, and all its nose rubbed off. My naughty little sister called *her* doll 'Rosy-primrose'. My little sister used to take Rosy-primrose to bed with her, but sometimes, when my naughty little sister was cross, she would smack poor Rosy-primrose and throw her out of bed.

One day, when my naughty little sister threw Rosy-primrose out of bed, my mother said, 'I think I'll take that poor old doll downstairs and put her in the cupboard until you can be kind to her.'

But my naughty little sister said, 'Won't be kind to her.' So my mother put Rosy-primrose away in the cupboard for a rest.

Now, what do you think? The very next day, when my mother was doing the ironing, she sud-

denly said, 'Where is that naughty little girl? Where is that naughty sister of yours? I expect she's in mischief, because she is so quiet.' That's what my mother said.

So my mother stopped her ironing, and went out into the garden to look for my little sister. But she wasn't in the garden. My mother looked in the shed, and she wasn't in the shed. She wasn't in the sitting-room, or in her bedroom, or in the spare room, but when my mother peeped into her own bedroom – there was my naughty little sister looking very cross at being caught.

The fairy-doll's box wasn't in the wardrobe drawer either. It was *on the bed*, and all the white paper was all over the floor, and there was my naughty little sister holding my fairy-doll and making it say, 'ma-ma, ma-ma, ma-ma, ma-ma.'

My mother was very cross. She said, 'That's not your doll. It belongs to your big sister,' and my naughty little sister said, 'I want it.' My mother said, 'Put it down on the bed,' and my very naughty little sister said, 'No.'

Then my mother was angry, and went to take the doll away from my naughty little sister, but that bad child ran away with my lovely fairy-doll. And, well – you remember what she did to poor Rosy-primrose when she was cross, don't you? She did something *even more dreadful* to my fairy-doll. *She threw it out of the window*, that lovely beautiful doll with the golden wings and the shiny crown *and* the sticking-out dress with golden stars on.

My naughty little sister had to go straight to bed for that, because she really had been terrible.

My lovely fairy-doll had fallen down into the garden, right into a muddy puddle, and its face was broken. I cried and cried, and when my little sister saw the poor fairy-doll, she cried and cried too, because she wasn't really such a bad child as all that – she just threw the doll out of the window when she was being mischievous.

My naughty little sister was so very sorry that we all forgave her, and my mother said that if she promised to be kind in future, she should have Rosy-primrose back very soon. So my little sister promised hard.

Do you know what my kind mother did? She sent the poor fairy-doll to the Doll's Hospital, and she sent Rosy-primrose there too, and when the two dolls came back, they looked very nice.

My little sister was a bit sorry to see Rosy-primrose, because Rosy-primrose had a new nice face and some curly hair that hadn't been there for a long, long time. My little sister never was quite happy with the tidy Rosy-primrose until it lost all its hair again, and its new eyes fell in. But she was always kind to it after that.

I was glad about my fairy-doll, though. Because it wasn't a fairy any more after the window-fall. It had a pretty new face, and a nice smile with teeth showing, and it *still* shut its eyes when you laid it down, and it *still* said, 'ma-ma'; but the fairy-clothes had all been spoiled in the muddy puddle, so my mother had made it a nice yellow dress and bonnet, and a white apron, and I called it 'Annabella,' and now that its clothes were not so grand, I could play with it whenever I wanted to – so really that fairy-doll's window-fall wasn't so terribly dreadful after all.

8

My Naughty Little Sister Cuts Out

ONCE, when I was a little girl, and my naughty little sister was a very little girl, it rained and rained and rained. It rained every day, and it rained all the time, and everything got wetter and wetter and wetter, and when my naughty little sister went out she had to wear her mackintosh and her wellingtons.

My naughty little sister had a beautiful red mackintosh-cape with a hood – just like Little Red Riding Hood's – and she had a little red umbrella. My little sister used to carry her umbrella under her cape, because she didn't want to get it wet. Wasn't she a silly girl?

When my naughty little sister went down the road, the rain went plop, plop, plop, plop, on to her head, and scatter-scatter-scatter against her cape, and trickle, trickle down her cheeks, and her wellington boots went splish-splosh, splish-splosh in the puddles.

My naughty little sister liked puddles very much, and she splished and sploshed such a lot that the water got into the tops of her wellingtons and made her feet wet inside, and then my naughty little sister was very sorry, because she caught a cold.

She got a nasty, sneezy, atishoo-y cold, and couldn't go out in the rain any more. My poor little sister looked very miserable when my mother said she could not go out. But her cold was very bad, and she had a red nose, and red eyes, and a nasty buzzy ear – all because of getting her feet wet, and every now and again – she couldn't help it – she said, 'A-A-tishoo!'

Now, my naughty little sister was a fidgety child. She wouldn't sit down quietly to hear a story like you do, or play nicely with a toy, or draw pictures with a pencil – she just fidgeted and wriggled and grumbled all the time, and said, 'Want to go out in the rain – want to splash and splash,' in the crossest and growliest voice, and then she said, 'A-a-tishoo!' even when she didn't want to, because of the nasty cold she'd got. And she grumbled and grumbled and grumbled.

My mother made her an orange-drink, but she grumbled. My mother gave her cough-stuff, but she grumbled, and really no one knew how to make her good.

My mother said, 'Why don't you look at a picture-book?'

And my naughty little sister said, 'No book, nasty book.'

Then my mother said, 'Well, would you like to play with my button-box?' and my naughty little sister said she thought she might like that. But when she had dropped all the buttons out and spilled them

all over the floor, she said, 'No buttons, tired of buttons. A-a-tishoo!' She said, 'A-a-tishoo' like that, because she couldn't help it.

My mother said, 'Dear me, what can I do for the child?'

Then my mother had a good idea. She said, 'I know, you can make a scrap-book!'

So my mother found a big book with clean pages, and a lot of old birthday cards and Christmas cards, and some old picture-books, and a big pot of sticky paste and she showed my naughty little sister how to make a scrap-book.

My naughty little sister was quite pleased, because she had never been allowed to use scissors before, and these were the nice snippy ones from mother's work-box.

My naughty little sister cut out a picture of a cow, and a basket with roses in, and a lady in a red dress, and a house and a squirrel, and she stuck them all in the big book with the sticky paste, and then she laughed and laughed.

Do you know why she laughed? She laughed because she had stuck them all in the book in a funny way. She stuck the lady in first, and then she put the basket of roses on the lady's head, and the cow on top of that, and then she put the house and the squirrel under the lady's feet. My naughty little sister thought that the lady looked very funny with the basket of flowers and the cow on her head.

So my naughty little sister amused herself for quite a long while, and my mother said, 'Thank goodness,' and went upstairs to tidy the bedrooms, as my naughty little sister wasn't grumbling any more.

But that naughty child soon got tired of the scrap-book, and when she got tired of it, she started rubbing the sticky paste over the table, and made the table all gummy. Wasn't that nasty of her?

Then she poked the scissors into the birthday cards and the Christmas cards, and made them look very ugly, and then, because she liked to do snip-snipping with the scissors, she looked round for something big to cut.

Fancy looking round for mischief like that! But she did. She didn't care at all, she just looked round for something to cut.

She snipped up all father's newspaper with the scissors, and she tried to snip the pussy-cat's tail, only pussy put her back up and said 'Pss', and frightened my naughty little sister.

So my naughty little sister looked round for something that she could cut up easily, and she found a big brown-paper parcel on a chair – a parcel all tied up with white string.

My naughty sister was so bad because she couldn't go out and play in the wet, that she cut the string of the parcel. She knew that she shouldn't, but she didn't care a bit. She cut the string right through, and pulled it all off. She did that because she thought it would be nice to cut up all the brown paper that was round the parcel.

So she dragged the parcel on to the floor, and began to pull off the brown paper. But when the brown paper was off, my very naughty little sister found something inside that she thought would be much nicer to cut. It was a lovely piece of silky, rustly material with little flowers all over it – the sort of special stuff that party-dresses are made of.

Now my naughty little sister knew that she mustn't cut stuff like that, but she didn't care. She thought she would just make a quick snip to see how it sounded when it was cut. So she did make a snip, and the stuff went 'scc-scrr-scrr' as the scissors bit it, and my naughty little sister was so pleased that she forgot about everything else, and just cut and cut.

And then, all of a sudden . . . yes! *In came my mother!*

My mother was cross when she saw the sticky table, and the cut-up newspaper, but when she looked on the floor and saw my naughty little sister cutting the silky stuff, she was very, very angry.

'You are a bad, bad child,' my mother said. 'You shall not have the scissors any more. Your kind Aunt Betty is going to be married soon, and she sent this nice stuff for me to make you a bridesmaid's dress, because she wanted you to hold up her dress in church for her. Now you won't be able to go.'

49

My naughty little sister cried and cried because she wanted to be a bridesmaid and because she liked to have new dresses very much. But it was no use, because the stuff was all cut up.

After that my naughty little sister tried to be a good girl until her cold was better.

9

My Naughty Little Sister
at the Party

YOU wouldn't think there could be another child as naughty as my naughty little sister, would you? But there was. There was a thoroughly bad boy who was my naughty little sister's best boy-friend, and this boy's name was Harry.

This Bad Harry and my naughty little sister used to play together quite a lot in Harry's garden, or in our garden, and got up to dreadful mischief between them, picking all the baby gooseberries, and the green black-currants, and throwing sand on the flower-beds, and digging up the runner-bean seeds, and all the naughty sorts of things you never, never do in the garden.

Now, one day this Bad Harry's birthday was near, and Bad Harry's mother said he could have a birthday-party and invite lots of children to tea. So Bad Harry came round to our house with a pretty card in an envelope for my naughty little sister, and this card was an invitation asking my naughty little sister to come to the birthday-party.

Bad Harry told my naughty little sister that there

would be a lovely tea with jellies and sandwiches and birthday-cake, and my naughty little sister said 'Jolly good.'

And every time she thought about the party she said, 'Nice tea and birthday-cake.' Wasn't she greedy? And when the party day came she didn't make any fuss when my mother dressed her in her

new green party-dress, and her green party-shoes and her green hair-ribbon, and she didn't fidget and she didn't wriggle her head about when she was having her hair combed, she kept as still as still, because she was so pleased to think about the party, and when my mother said, 'Now, what must you say at the party?' My naughty little sister said, 'I must say, "nice tea".'

But my mother said, 'No, no, that *would* be a greedy thing to say. You must say "please" and "thank you", like a good polite child, at tea-time, and say, "thank you very much for having me", when the party is over.'

And my naughty little sister said, 'All right, Mother, I promise.'

So, my mother took my naughty little sister to the party, and what do you think the silly little girl did as soon as she got there? She went up to Bad Harry's mother and she said very quickly, 'Please-and-thank-you, and-thank-you-very-much-for-having me,' all at once – just like that, before she forgot to be polite, and then she said, 'Now may I have a lovely tea?'

Wasn't that rude and greedy? Bad Harry's mother said, 'I'm afraid you will have to wait until all the other children are here, but Harry shall show you the tea-table if you like.'

Bad Harry looked very smart in a blue party-suit, with white socks and shoes and a *real man's haircut*, and he said, 'Come on, I'll show you.'

So they went into the tea-room and there was the birthday-tea spread out on the table. Bad Harry's mother had made red jellies and yellow jellies, and blancmanges, and biscuits, and sandwiches, and cakes-with-cherries-on, and a big birthday-cake with white icing on it and candles, and 'Happy Birthday Harry', written on it.

My naughty little sister's eyes grew bigger and bigger, and Bad Harry said, 'There's something else in the larder. It's going to be a surprise treat, but you shall see it because you are my best girl-friend.'

So Bad Harry took my naughty little sister out

into the kitchen and they took chairs and climbed up to the larder shelf – which is a dangerous thing to do, and it would have been their own faults if they had fallen down – and Bad Harry showed my naughty little sister a lovely spongy trifle, covered with creamy stuff and with silver balls and jelly-sweets on the top. And my naughty little sister stared more than ever because she liked spongy trifle better than jellies, or blancmanges, or biscuits, or sand-wiches, or cakes-with-cherries-on, or even birthday-cake, so she said, 'For me.'

Bad Harry said, 'For me too,' because he liked spongy trifle best as well.

Then Bad Harry's mother called to them and said, 'Come along, the other children are arriving.'

So they went to say, 'How do you do!' to the other children, and then Bad Harry's mother said, 'I think we will have a few games now before tea – just until everyone has arrived.'

All the other children stood in a ring and Bad Harry's mother said, 'Ring O'Roses first, I think.' And all the nice party children said, 'Oh, we'd like that.'

But my naughty little sister said, 'No Ring O'Roses – nasty Ring O'Roses' – just like that, because she didn't like Ring O'Roses very much, and Bad Harry said, 'Silly game.' So Bad Harry and my naughty little sister stood and watched the others. The other children sang beautifully too, they sang:

> 'Ring O'Ring O'Roses,
> A pocket full of posies –
> A-tishoo, a-tishoo, we all fall down.'

And they all fell down and laughed, but Harry and my naughty little sister didn't laugh. They got tired of watching and they went for a little walk. Do you know where they went to?

Yes. To the larder. To take another look at the spongy trifle. They climbed up on to the chairs to look at it really properly. It was very pretty.

'Ring O'Ring O'Roses' sang the good party children.

'Nice jelly-sweets,' said my naughty little sister. 'Nice silver balls,' and she looked at that terribly Bad Harry and he looked at her.

'Take one,' said that naughty boy, and my naughty little sister did take one, she took a red jelly-sweet from the top of the trifle; and then Bad Harry took a green jelly-sweet; and then my naughty little sister took a yellow jelly-sweet and a silver ball, and then Bad Harry took three jelly-sweets, red, green and yellow, and six silver balls. One, two, three, four, five, six, and put them all in his mouth at once.

Now some of the creamy stuff had come off upon Bad Harry's fingers and he had licked it and liked it very much, so he put his finger into the creamy stuff on the trifle, and took some of it off and ate it, and my naughty little sister ate some too. I'm sorry to have to tell you this, because I feel so ashamed of them, and expect you feel ashamed of them too.

I hope you aren't too shocked to hear any more? Because, do you know, those two bad children forgot all about the party and the nice children all singing 'Ring O'Roses'. They took a spoon each and scraped off the creamy stuff and ate it, and then they began to eat the nice spongy inside.

Bad Harry said, 'Now we've made the trifle look so untidy, no one else will want any, so we may as well eat it all up.' So they dug away into the spongy inside of the trifle and found lots of nice fruity bits inside. It was a very big trifle, but those greedy children ate and ate.

Then just as they had nearly finished the whole big trifle, the 'Ring O'Roses'-ing stopped and Bad Harry's mother called, 'Where are you two? We are ready for tea.'

Then my naughty little sister was very frightened. Because she knew she had been very naughty, and she looked at Bad Harry and *he* knew *he* had been very naughty, and they both felt terrible. Bad Harry had a creamy mess of trifle all over his face, and even in his real man's haircut, and my naughty little sister had made her new green party-dress all trifly – you know how it happens if you eat too quickly and greedily.

'It's tea-time,' said Bad Harry, and he looked at my naughty little sister, and my naughty little sister thought of the jellies and the cakes and the sandwiches, and all the other things, and she felt very full of trifle, and she said, 'Don't want any.'

And do you know what she did? Just as Bad Harry's mother came into the kitchen, my naughty little sister slipped out of the door, and ran and ran all the way home. It was a good thing our home was only down the street and no roads to cross, or I don't know what would have happened to her.

Bad Harry's mother was so cross when she saw the trifle, that she sent Bad Harry straight to bed, and he had to stay there and hear all the nice children enjoying themselves. I don't know what happened to him in the night, but I know that my naughty little sister wasn't at all a well girl, from having eaten so much trifle – and I also know that she doesn't like spongy trifle any more.

10

The Naughtiest Story of All

THIS is such a very terrible story about my naughty little sister that I hardly know how to tell it to you. It is all about one Christmas-time when I was a little girl, and my naughty little sister was a very little girl.

Now, my naughty little sister was very pleased when Christmas began to draw near, because she liked all the excitement of the plum-puddings and the turkeys, and the crackers and the holly, and all the Christmassy-looking shops, but there was one very awful thing about her – she didn't like to think about Father Christmas at all – she said he was a *horrid old man*!

There – I knew you would be shocked at that. But she did. And she said she wouldn't put up her stocking for him.

My mother told my naughty little sister what a good old man Father Christmas was, and how he brought the toys along on Christmas Eve, but my naughty little sister said, 'I don't care. And I don't want that nasty old man coming to our house.'

Well now, that was bad enough, wasn't it? But the really dreadful thing happened later on.

This is the dreadful thing: one day, my school-teacher said that a Father Christmas Man would be coming to the school to bring presents for all the children, and my teacher said that the Father Christmas Man would have toys for all our little brothers and sisters as well, if they cared to come along for them. She said that there would be a real Christmas-tree with candles on it, and sweeties and cups of tea and biscuits for our mothers.

Wasn't that a nice thought? Well now, when I told my little sister about the Christmas-tree, she said, 'Oh, nice!'

And when I told her about the sweeties she said, 'Very, very nice!' But when I told her about the Father Christmas Man, she said, 'Don't want *him*, nasty old man.'

Still, my mother said, 'You can't go to the Christmas-tree without seeing him, so if you don't want to see him all that much, you will have to stay at home.'

But my naughty little sister did want to go, very much, so she said, 'I will go, and when the horrid Father Christmas Man comes in, I will close my eyes.'

So, we all went to the Christmas-tree together, my mother and I, and my naughty little sister.

When we got to the school, my naughty little sister was very pleased to see all the pretty paperchains that we had made in school hanging all round the class-rooms, and when she saw all the little lanterns, and the holly and all the robin-redbreast drawings pinned on the blackboards she smiled and smiled. She was very smily at first.

All the mothers, and the little brothers and sisters who were too young for school sat down in chairs and desks, and the big school-children acted a play for them.

My little sister was very excited to see all the children dressed up as fairies and robins and elves and bo-peeps and things, and she clapped her hands very hard, like all the grown-ups did, to show that she was enjoying herself. And she still smiled.

Then, when some of the teachers came round with bags of sweets, tied up in pretty coloured paper, my little sister smiled even more, and she sang too when all the children sang. She sang, 'Away in a manger', because she knew the words very well. When she didn't know the words of some of the singing, she 'la-la'd'.

After all the singing, the teachers put out the lights, and took away a big screen from a corner of the room, and there was the Christmas-tree, all lit up with candles and shining with silvery stuff, and little shiny coloured balls. There were lots of toys on the tree, and all the children cheered and clapped.

Then the teachers put the light on again, and blew out the candles, so that we could all go and look at the tree. My little sister went too. She looked at the tree, and she looked at the toys, and she saw a specially nice doll with a blue dress on, and she said, 'For me.'

My mother said, 'You must wait and see what you are given.'

Then the teachers called out, 'Back to your seats, everyone, we have a visitor coming.' So all the children went back to their seats, and sat still and waited and listened.

And, as we waited and listened, we heard a tinkle-tinkle bell noise, and then the schoolroom door opened, and in walked the Father Christmas Man. My naughty little sister had forgotten all about him, so she hadn't time to close her eyes before he walked in. However, when she saw him, my little sister stopped smiling and began to be stubborn.

The Father Christmas Man was very nice. He said he hoped we were having a good time, and we all said, 'Yes,' except my naughty little sister – she didn't say a thing.

Then he said, 'Now, come up one at a time, children; and I will give each one of you a toy.'

So, first of all each school-child went up for a toy, and my naughty little sister still didn't shut her eyes because she wanted to see who was going to have the specially nice doll in the blue dress. But none of the school-children had it.

Then Father Christmas began to call the little brothers and sisters up for presents, and, as he didn't know their names, he just said, 'Come along, sonny,' if it were a boy, and 'come along, girlie,' if it were a girl. The Father Christmas Man let the little brothers and sisters choose their own toys off the tree.

When my naughty little sister saw this, she was so worried about the specially nice doll, that she thought that she would just go up and get it. She said, 'I don't like that horrid old beardy man, but I do like that nice doll.'

So, my naughty little sister got up without being asked to, and she went right out to the front where the Father Christmas Man was standing, and she said, 'That doll, please,' and pointed to the doll she wanted.

The Father Christmas Man laughed and all the teachers laughed, and the other mothers and the school-children, and all the little brothers and sisters. My mother did not laugh because she was so shocked to see my naughty little sister going out without being asked to.

The Father Christmas Man took the specially nice doll off the tree, and he handed it to my naughty little sister and he said, 'Well now, I hear you don't like me very much, but won't you just shake hands?'

and my naughty little sister said, 'No.' But she took the doll all the same.

The Father Christmas Man put out his nice old hand for her to shake and be friends, and do you know what that naughty bad girl did? *She bit his hand.* She really and truly did. Can you think of anything more dreadful and terrible? She bit Father Christmas's good old hand, and then she turned and ran and ran out of the school with all the children staring after her, and her doll held very tight in her arms.

The Father Christmas Man was very nice, he said it wasn't a hard bite, only a frightened one, and he made all the children sing songs together.

When my naughty little sister was brought back by my mother, she said she was very sorry, and the Father Christmas Man said, 'That's all right, old lady,' and because he was so smily and nice to her, my funny little sister went right up to him, and gave him a big 'sorry' kiss, which pleased him very much.

And she hung her stocking up after all, and that kind man remembered to fill it for her.

My little sister kept the specially nice doll until she was quite grown-up. She called it Rosy-primrose, and although she was sometimes bad-tempered with it, she really loved it very much indeed.

11

My Naughty Little Sister
does Knitting

ONE day, when I was a little girl, and my naughty little sister was another little girl, a kind lady came to live next door to us. This kind lady's really true name was Mrs Jones, but my little sister always called her Mrs Cocoa Jones.

Do you know why she called her that? Shall I tell you? *Well*, it was because Mrs Cocoa Jones used to give my naughty little sister a cup of cocoa every morning.

Yes, every single morning, when it was eleven o'clock, Mrs Cocoa Jones used to bang hard on her kitchen wall with the handle of her floor-brush, and as our kitchen was right the other side of the wall, my naughty little sister could hear very well, and would bang and bang back to show that she was quite ready.

Then, my little sister would go into Mrs Cocoa Jones's house to drink cocoa with her. Wasn't that a nice idea?

My little sister used to go in to see Mrs Cocoa Jones so much that Mr Cocoa Jones made a little low gate between his garden and our father's garden so that my little sister could pop in without having to go all round the front of the house each time. Mr Cocoa Jones made a nice little archway over the gate, and planted a little rose-tree to climb over it, especially for her. Wasn't she a fortunate child?

So you see, Mrs Cocoa Jones was a very great friend.

Well now, Mrs Cocoa Jones was a lady who was always knitting and knitting, and as she hadn't any

little boys and girls of her own, she used to knit a lot of lovely woollies for my naughty little sister, and for me.

She knitted us red jumpers and blue jumpers, and yellow jumpers and red caps and blue caps and yellow caps to match, and she also knitted a blue jumper for Rosy-primrose, who was my naughty little sister's favourite doll, and when she had finished all the caps and jumpers, she made us lots of pairs of socks. So, every time we saw Mrs Cocoa, she always had a bag of wool and a lot of clicky needles.

Sometimes, when Mrs Cocoa Jones wanted the wool wound up, she would ask my naughty little sister to hold it for her, and that fidgety child would drop it and tangle it, until Mr Cocoa Jones used to say, 'It looks to me as if you will be doing *knotting* not knitting with that lot,' to Mrs Cocoa. And my funny little sister would laugh and laugh because she thought it very funny to say 'knotting' like that.

Now, one day Mrs Cocoa Jones said, 'Would you like to learn to knit?' to my naughty little sister.

'Would you like to learn to knit?' she asked my little sister, and my little sister said, 'Not very much.'

Then Mrs Cocoa said, 'Well, but think of all the nice things you could make for everyone. You could knit Christmas presents and birthday presents all by yourself.'

Then my naughty little sister thought it would be rather nice to learn to knit, so she said, 'All right then, Mrs Cocoa Jones, would you please teach me?'

So Mrs Cocoa Jones lent her a pair of rather bendy needles and she gave her some wool, and she showed her how to knit. So, carefully, carefully my little sister learned to put the wool round the needle, and carefully, carefully to bring it out and make a stitch, and carefully, carefully to make another until she could really truly knit.

Then my naughty little sister was very pleased, because she had a good idea. She thought that as

67

Mr Cocoa Jones had made her such a nice little gate, she would knit him a new scarf for his birthday, because his old scarf had got all moth-holey. The naughty little baby moths had eaten bits of scarf and made holes in it, so my little sister thought he would like a new one very much.

She didn't tell anyone about it. Not even Mrs Cocoa Jones, she wanted it to be a real secret.

Well now, Mrs Cocoa had given my little sister all her odds and endsy bits of wool, the red bits and the blue bits and the yellow bits from our jumpers, and some grey and purple and white and black and brown bits as well, so my little sister thought she would make a beautiful scarf.

She went secretly, secretly into corners to knit this beautiful scarf for Mr Cocoa Jones's birthday. Wasn't she a clever child?

She kept it carefully hidden all the time she wasn't making it. She hid it in lots of funny places too. She hid it under her pillow, and in the coal-shed and behind the settee, and in the flour-tub. But most of the time she was knitting and knitting to have it made in time. So that, when Mr Cocoa Jones's birthday did come, it was quite ready and quite finished.

It was a very pretty scarf because of all the pretty colours my little sister had used, and although it was a bit coaly and a bit floury here and there, it still looked very lovely, and Mr Cocoa Jones was very pleased with it.

He said, 'It's the best scarf I have ever had!'

Then my little sister told him all about how she had knitted it, and she showed him some holes in it too, where the stitches had dropped, and Mr Cocoa Jones said they would make nice homes for the baby moths to live in anyway, so my little sister was glad she had dropped the stitches.

Then Mr Cocoa Jones said that as it was the very nicest scarf he had ever had knitted for him, it would be a shame to waste it by wearing it every day. He said he would get Mrs Cocoa to put it away for him for High Days and Holidays.

So Mrs Cocoa wrapped it up very neatly and nicely in blue laundry paper, and she let my little sister put it away in Mr Cocoa's drawer for him, and Mr Cocoa wore his old scarf for every day until Mrs Cocoa had time to knit him another one.

12

My Naughty Little Sister goes
to the Pantomime

A LONG time ago, when I was a little girl, and my little sister was a little girl too, my mother took us to see the Christmas Pantomime.

The Pantomime was in a Theatre, which was a very beautiful place with red tippy-up seats and a lot of ladies and gentlemen playing music in front of the curtains.

My little sister was a very good quiet child at first, because she had never been to the Pantomime before. She sat very still and mousy. She didn't say anything. She just looked and looked.

She looked at the lights, and the lots and lots of seats, and the music-people and the other boys and girls. She didn't even fidget at first, because she wasn't quite sure about the tippy-up seat.

When we were in the Theatre, our mother gave us a bag of sweets each. I had chocolate-creams, and my little sister had toffee-drops, because she liked them so much, but she was so quiet that she didn't eat even a single one of them before the Pantomime started.

She just held the sweeties on her lap, so that when the music man who plays the cymbals suddenly made them go 'Rish-tish a-tish!' and the curtains came back, she was so surprised that she dropped them all over the floor, and my mother had to pick them up for her.

My little sister was so surprised because she hadn't known that Pantomime was people dancing and singing and falling over things, but when she saw that it was, she was very excited, and when the other children clapped their hands, she clapped hers very hard too.

At first, my little sister was so surprised that she liked every bit of it, but after a while she said her favourite was the fat funny man. The play was all about the Babes in the Wood, and the fat funny man was called Humpty Dumpty. He was very funny indeed, and when he came on, he always said, 'Hallo, boys and girls.'

And the boys and girls said, 'Hallo, Humpty Dumpty.'

And he said, 'How are you tomorrow?' and we said, 'We are very well today.' He told us to say this every time, and we never forgot. Once, my little sister shouted so loud, '*Hallo, Humpty Dumpty*.' She shouted 'HALLO, HUMPTY DUMPTY,' like that, that Humpty Dumpty heard her, and he waved specially to her. My goodness, wasn't she a proud girl then!

The other thing my little sister liked was the fairies dancing. There were lots of fairies in the Pantomime, and they had lovely sparkly dresses, and when they danced the lights went red and blue and green, and some of them *really flew* right up in the air!

Humpty Dumpty tried to fly too, but he fell right over and bumped his nose. My naughty little sister was so sorry for him, that she began to cry and cry, really true tear-crying, not just howling.

But when Humpty Dumpty jumped up and said, 'Hallo, boys and girls,' and we all said, 'Hallo, Humpty Dumpty,' and when he began to dance again, she knew he wasn't really hurt so she laughed and laughed.

And presently, what do you think? My little sister had a really exciting thing happen.

Humpty Dumpty came on to the stage and he sang a little song for all the boys and girls, and then he made all the children sing too. After that he said, 'Would any little boy or girl like to come up on the stage and dance with me?' And do you know what my little sister said, 'Yes, I will. I will.' And she ran out of her seat and up the stage steps and right on to the big theatre stage before my mother could do anything about it.

All the people cheered and clapped when my

little sister ran up on to the stage, and a lot of other boys and girls went up too then, and soon they were all dancing with Humpty Dumpty. Round and round and up and down, until two ladies dressed like men came on the stage.

Then Humpty Dumpty said, 'All right, children, down you go,' and all the boys and girls went down again, off the stage and back to their mothers.

All except my bad little sister. *Because she wasn't there*. She'd vanished! And what do you think?

While the two ladies dressed like men were singing on the stage, the funny man came back, with my little sister sitting on his shoulder. And he came right off the stage and down the steps and brought her back to mother, and my little sister looked very pleased and smily.

All the people stared and stared to see my naughty little sister being carried back by Humpty Dumpty. Even the singing ladies dressed like men stared.

And do you know where she had been?

The bad child had slipped round the side of the stage while the other children were dancing, to see if she could find the fairies!

And she did find them too. She said they were drinking lemonade and they gave her some as well.

It wasn't very fairyish lemonade, she said, it was the fizzy nose-tickle sort.

She told us another thing too, a secret thing. She said they weren't real true fairies, only little girls like herself, and she said that when she was a bit older she was going to be a stage fairy like those little girls.

13

My Naughty Little Sister
goes to School

ONE day, when I was a little girl, my mother had a letter from my grannie, to say that she was ill in bed, and would mother come over for a day to see her?

So my mother wrote a letter to my school-teacher to ask if my little sister could come to school with me next day, as grannie was ill. My teacher said, 'Yes, she can come if she will be good.' And wasn't my funny little sister pleased!

Do you know what she did? She found an old case belonging to my father, and she put in it all the things she thought she would want for school next day. She put in a pencil and a rubber, and some crayons, and some story-books, and an apple, and a matchbox, and Rosy-primrose who was her doll.

Then she went to bed very quickly like a good girl. She didn't splash about in the bath, or scream when she had her hair done, or grumble about her supper, or say her prayers naughtily, or worry and worry for lots of stories in bed. No. She shut her eyes quickly so as to go to sleep and make tomorrow come as soon as soon. That's what the sensible child did.

And in the morning, she got up early, and she *dressed herself.* Yes! Even the *buttons*, and her socks! To show the teacher how nicely she could do it.

Then, while our mother was getting the breakfast ready, she went out into the garden, and she picked a nice bunch of flowers out of her own garden for the teacher. So for once in a while she was my good little sister.

Well now, when my little sister got to school, she was still being very good. She said, 'Good morning,' to everyone and she came nicely into school, and because she looked so good and special the teacher said she could sit next to me all day.

So my little sister sat down right next to me,

and stared and stared at all the other children in the room, and when she saw them opening their bags and cases and getting out their books and pencil-boxes, she opened her case and took out all her things too. She took out the pencil and the rubber, and the crayons and the story-books but she left the apple and the matchbox and Rosy-primrose in the case because she wanted them for play-time.

When school started, my little sister stood up very straight to sing the school hymns, and she shut her eyes very tight for the school prayers, and then she sat down as good as good, nice and straight like the teacher told us to.

Then the teacher called all the children's names, and when each child's name was called, the child said, 'Present.' My naughty little sister was very surprised, and when my name was called I said, 'Present,' too. But the teacher didn't call my little sister's name, because she wasn't a real school-child, and do you know what my naughty little sister did?

She forgot to be a good child, and she started to shout, 'I want a present, I want a present.' Wasn't she silly?

But after that my little sister was very good again, and the teacher let her play with some plasticine. My little sister made a red basket with the plasticine, and the teacher said it was very good, and put it on the mantelpiece for everyone to see.

Then our teacher read us a story, and my little sister was very interested, and when our teacher asked questions about the story, and all the children put their hands up, my little sister put her hand up too, and all the children laughed. But our teacher said they mustn't laugh, and she asked my little sister a real big-child's question about the story, and my little sister gave the *right answer*. Then our teacher said, as my little sister was such a clever child she could have ten out of ten. (You know ten out of ten is a very big thing to have at school.)

So our teacher wrote 'Ten out of ten' on a piece of paper for my little sister and put it on the mantelpiece for her with the plasticine basket, and my little sister was a very proud child.

When dinner-time came, our teacher let my little sister sit with her, and my little sister was so good that the teacher said all the other children should try to be like her. Wasn't she behaving well?

In the afternoon we drew pictures with our crayons, and my little sister drew a picture with her crayons. She was very pleased to think she had brought her own crayons to school.

I drew a little house, and a tree and a pond, and some little people. But do you know what my little sister drew? She drew the teacher, and all the school-children! Yes, all of them in the class. The teacher was very pleased to see such a lovely drawing, because my little sister had not forgotten anything – she had even put in her plasticine basket and her ten out of ten writing. So Teacher said the drawing must go on the mantelpiece with the other clever things. My little sister drew in her drawing very small next to the plasticine basket, and then the picture was put up for everyone to see.

Then we all went out into the playground and did drill, and my little sister did drill as well, and she stood so straight, and put her arms so nicely that teacher let her do it in front of all the class.

So you see, she was being a very good child.

When we went back into school though, and did reading, my little sister got very quiet, and very still, and do you know what happened? She fell fast asleep in the desk. She slept and slept right until our mother came to fetch us home, and, because she had been so good and no trouble, our teacher let her take home the lovely drawing, and the plasticine basket, and the ten out of ten paper.

14

When my Father minded my
Naughty Little Sister

WHEN my sister was a naughty little girl, she had a very cross friend. My little sister's cross friend was called Mr Blakey, and he was a very grumbly old man.

My little sister's friend Mr Blakey was the shoe-mender man, and he had a funny little shop with bits of leather all over the floor, and boxes of nails, and boot-polish, and shoe-laces, all over the place. Mr Blakey had a picture in his shop too. It was a very beautiful picture of a little dog with boots on all four feet, walking in the rain. My little sister loved that picture very much, but she loved Mr Blakey better than that.

Every time we went into Mr Blakey's shop with our mother, my naughty little sister would start meddling with things, and Mr Blakey would say, 'Leave that be, you varmint,' in a very loud cross voice, and my little sister would stop meddling at once, just like an obedient child, because Mr Blakey was her favourite man, and one day, when we went into his shop, do you know what she did? She went straight behind the counter and kissed him *without being asked*. Mr Blakey was very surprised because he had a lot of nails in his mouth, but after that, he always gave her a peppermint humbug after he had shouted at her.

Well, that's about Mr Blakey in case you wonder who he was later on, now this is the real story:

One day, my mother had to go out shopping, so she asked my father if he would mind my naughty little sister for the day. My mother said she would take me shopping because I was a big girl, but my little sister was too draggy and moany to go to the big shops.

My father said he would mind my little sister, but my little sister said, 'I want to go, I want to go.' You know how she said that by now, I think. 'I want to go' – like that. And she kicked and screamed.

My mother said, 'Oh, dear, how tiresome you are,' to my little sister, but my father said, 'You'll jolly well do as you're told, old lady.'

Then my naughty little sister wouldn't eat her breakfast, but my mother went off shopping with me just the same, and when we had gone, my father looked very fierce, and he said, 'What about that breakfast?'

So my naughty little sister ate all her breakfast up, every bit, and she said, 'More milk, please,' and 'more bread, please', so much that my father got tired getting it for her.

Then, as it was a hot day, my father said, 'I'll bring my work into the garden, and give an eye to you at the same time.'

So my father took a chair and a table out into the garden, and my little sister went out into the garden too, and because my father was there she played good child's games. She didn't tread on the baby seedlings, or pick the flowers, or steal the black-currants, or do anything at all wicked. She didn't want my father to look fierce again, and my father said she was a good nice child.

My little sister just sat on the lawn and played with Rosy-primrose, and she made a tea-party with leaves and nasturtium seeds, and when she wanted something she asked my father for it nicely, not going off and finding it for herself at all.

She said, 'Please, Father, would you get me Rosy-primrose's box?' and my father put down his pen, and his writing-paper, and got out of his chair, and went and got Rosy-primrose's box, which was on the top shelf of the toy-cupboard and had all Rosy-primrose's tatty old clothes in it.

Then my father did writing again, and then my little sister said, 'Please can I have a drink of water?' She said it nicely, 'Please,' she said.

That was very good of her to ask, because she

sometimes used to drink germy water out of the water-butt, but father wasn't pleased at all, he said, 'Bother!' because he was being a busy man, and he stamped and stamped to the kitchen to get the water for my polite little sister.

But my father didn't know about Rosy-primrose's water. You see, when my little sister had a drink she always gave Rosy-primrose a drink too in a blue doll's cup. So when my father brought back the water, my little sister said, 'Where is Rosy-primrose's water?' and my cross father said, 'Bother Rosy-primrose,' like that, cross and grumbly.

And my father was crosser and grumblier when my little sister asked him to put Rosy-primrose's box back in the toy-cupboard, he said, 'That wretched doll again?' and he took Rosy-primrose and shut her in the box too, and put it on top of the bookcase, to show how firm he was going to be. So then my little sister stopped being good.

She started to yell and stamp, and make such a noise that people going by looked over the hedge to see what the matter was. Wouldn't you have been ashamed if it were you stamping and yelling with people looking at you? My naughty little sister wasn't ashamed. *She* didn't care about the people at all, she was a stubborn bad child.

My father was a stubborn man too. He took his table and his chair and his writing things indoors, and shut himself away in his study. 'You'll jolly well stay there till you behave,' he said to my naughty little sister.

My naughty little sister cried and cried until my father looked out of the window and said, 'Any more of that, and off to bed you go.' Then she was quiet, because she didn't want to go to bed.

She only peeped in once after that, but my father said, 'Go away, do,' and went on writing and writing, and he was so interested in his writing, he forgot all about my little sister, and it wasn't until he began to get hungry that he remembered her at all.

Then my father went out into the kitchen, and there was a lot of nice salad-stuff in the kitchen that our mother had left for lunch, there was junket too, and stewed pears, and biscuits for my father's and my little sister's lunches. My father remembered my little sister then, and he went to call her for lunch, because it was quite late. It was so late it was *four o'clock*.

But my little sister wasn't in the garden. My father looked and looked. He looked among the marrows, and behind the runner-bean rows, and under the hedge. He looked in the shed and down the cellar-hole, but there was no little girl.

Then my father went indoors again and looked all over the house, and all the time he was calling and calling, but there was still no little girl at all.

Then my father got worried. He didn't stop to change his slippers or eat his lunch. He went straight out of the gate, and down the road to look for my little sister. But he couldn't see her at all. He asked people, 'Have you seen a little girl with red hair?' and people said, 'No.'

My father was just coming up the road again, looking so hot and so worried, when my mother and I got off the bus. When my mother saw him, she said, 'He's lost that child,' because she knew my father and my little sister rather well.

When we got indoors my mother said, 'Why haven't you eaten your lunch?' and then my father told her all about the writing, and my bad sister. So my mother said, 'Well, if she's anywhere, she's near food of some kind, have you looked in the larder?' My father said he had. So mother said, 'Well, I don't know –'

Then I said something clever. I said, 'I expect she is with old Mr Blakey.' So we went off to Mr Blakey's shop, and there she was. Fast asleep on a pile of leather bits.

Mr Blakey seemed quite cross with us for having lost her, and my naughty little sister was very cross when we took her away because she said she had had a lovely time with Mr Blakey. Mr Blakey had boiled her an egg in his tea-kettle, and given her some bread and cheese out of newspaper, and let her cut it for herself with one of his nice leathery knives. Mother was cross because she had been looking forward to a nice cup of tea after the bus journey, and I was cross because my little sister had had such a fine time in Mr Blakey's shop.

The only happy one was my father. He said, 'Thank goodness I can work again without having to con-cen-trate on a disagreeable baby.' However, that made my little sister cry again, so he wasn't happy for long.

15

My Naughty Little Sister and the
Good Polite Child

ONCE, a long time ago, when I was little, my
mother said to my naughty little sister, 'I have a
little girl coming to tea this afternoon. I hope you
will be good and kind to her, because I am going to
mind her while her mother goes out.'

My little sister was very interested about this little
girl, and my mother said, 'Her name is Winnie and
she is a good polite child, I hear.'

So my little sister got all her toys out and put them
in the garden to show Winnie when she came, and
my mother made some cherry cakes and jam-tarts,
and some ginger biscuits for tea.

Wasn't my mother a kind woman, making
those nice things for tea? Do you know, because
Winnie was coming, my mother said, 'We will
have tea in the garden, with the best bluebird tablecloth.'

My little sister liked this, because the bluebird
tablecloth was very special. It had bluebirds on it,
and trees on it, and little funny men walking on
bridges on it, and little boats with men fishing on it,

and they were all blue as blue. My little sister said, 'I shall like that.'

When it was time for Winnie to come, my mother changed my little sister's dress, and put her on a pair of nice blue socks. My little sister was very proud of those blue socks, and when she heard the knock at the front door she ran to show them to the good polite Winnie.

But what do you think? Winnie had blue socks too! And a blue silky dress, and blue shiny shoes, and when she came in, her mother put her a frilly white silky apron on to keep her dress clean. My little sister was so pleased to see how pretty Winnie looked that she forgot to say, 'How do you do?' She said, 'Blue socks too?' instead.

But do you know, that Winnie didn't say anything! She just stood and stood, and she didn't look at our mother, or my little sister, she just peeped. She made her eyes all peepy and small, because she didn't like to look at anyone, and when her mother went away, she didn't scream for her, or shout, 'Good-bye,' to her, or make any noise and fuss of any kind. She just went on being thoroughly peepy, and she went quietly, quietly into the garden with my little sister without saying anything at all.

My little sister showed Winnie all her toys. She showed her Rosy-primrose first. Rosy-primrose wasn't very beautiful that day, because it was a time when she had lost her hair and her eyes, and Winnie just peeped at Rosy-primrose and didn't say anything.

So my little sister showed her the bricks, and the story-books, and the teddies, and the patty tins, and the tea-set, and the jig-saws, and all the other toys, and the good polite child didn't say anything at all.

So my funny little sister said, 'Can you talk?' and then Winnie said, 'Yes,' to show she could speak, so my little sister said, 'Would you like to make mud-pies?'

That good Winnie said, 'Oh, no, I might get dirty.' She didn't say 'Yes' because she didn't want to get her beautiful dress and her beautiful apron dirty, so my little sister said, 'Well, shall we go down the garden and eat gooseberries?' even though she knew that was naughty.

But good Winnie said, 'No, I might get tummy-ache.'

So my little sister said, 'Shall we have a race round the lawn?' and Winnie said, 'Oh, no, it's *so* hot,' in a quiet good voice.

And she didn't want to climb up the apple-trees in case she tore her frock, and she didn't want to sit on the grass in case there were ants, and she didn't want to shout over the front gate to the school-children because it was rude, and all the time she just looked peepy, peepy at my little sister.

So then my little sister said, 'What would you like to do?' And the polite good Winnie said she would like to take a story-book indoors to read. So she took one of the story-books indoors and read it on her own.

My naughty little sister didn't want to read story-books indoors, so she went and made a dirt pie, and ate some gooseberries, and raced round the lawn, and climbed the apple-trees, and sat on the grass, and then she shouted over the gate at the school-children, just to show how bad she could be.

When tea-time came, with all the nice cherry cakes and jam-tarts and ginger biscuits, the good polite Winnie came out and sat in the garden. When my little sister showed her the bluebird tablecloth Winnie only peeped and said, 'My mother has a tablecloth with roses and pansies and forget-me-nots on.'

And when my mother asked her to have a cake, she said, 'No, thank you, bread and butter, please,' and she wouldn't have a jam-tart, she had one little ginger biscuit, and then she said she wasn't hungry any more. Wasn't she polite?

My little sister wasn't polite like that. She had four cakes and three jam-tarts, and eight ginger biscuits. One, two, three, four, five, six, seven, eight, like that – and she ate them all up.

After tea good polite Winnie's mother came to fetch her home. She took off Winnie's apron and Winnie said, 'Good-bye, and thank you for minding me,' in a quiet good voice like that, 'Good afternoon,' she said.

When she had gone, my mother said, 'What a quiet child.' But what do you think my funny little sister said? She said, 'I'm glad I'm not as good as all that.'

And my mother said, 'Oh, well, you are not so bad, I suppose.'

16

My Naughty Little Sister and
Poor Charlie Cocoa

IN the days when I was a little girl, and my naughty little sister was a very small child, my little sister often helped Mrs Cocoa Jones to do her housework.

Mrs Cocoa worked *so* hard, and had SUCH a very clean and tidy house, that she was glad when my little sister came to help her.

Mrs Cocoa Jones had a shiny red dustpan and a brush with a red handle, and because my little sister was such a helpful child, Mrs Cocoa bought her a nice little shiny red dustpan and a little brush with a red handle for herself. Wasn't that very kind of her?

Mrs Cocoa hung her dustpan and brush on a hook behind her broom-cupboard door when she wasn't using them, and dear Mr Cocoa put another hook behind the broom-cupboard door so that my little sister could hang her dustpan and brush there too. It was a nice low hook so that my little sister could reach it all by herself. What a smily pleased girl she was when she saw her own little dustpan and brush hanging underneath Mrs Cocoa's big dustpan and brush!

'Now we shall WORK and WORK, Mrs Cocoa,' my little sister said.

When Mrs Cocoa swept her carpets, she knelt on the floor and brushed the dust into her dustpan, and my little sister knelt on the floor too, and brushed the dust into *her* dustpan. 'SWEEP SWEEP' went Mrs Cocoa's big brush and 'sweep sweep' went my little sister's small brush. 'AREN'T we busy, Mrs Cocoa?' said my little sister as she brushed and brushed.

Mrs Cocoa would sit up and say, 'Oh! my *poor* back!' and my naughty little sister would sit up and say, 'Oh, *my* poor back!' and then they would carry their pans of dust out to the dustbin and grumble and grumble about HARD WORK.

My little sister was only pretending to grumble, because she liked helping Mrs Cocoa and her back wasn't really bad at all, but poor Mrs Cocoa really was grumbling when she said 'Oh my *poor* back!'

Now, kind Mr Cocoa was very worried about Mrs Cocoa's poor back, so one day he took some money out of his savings and bought Mrs Cocoa a fine vacuum cleaner.

Mrs Cocoa *was* pleased! She had never had a vacuum cleaner before, and when Mr Cocoa fixed it up for her, and showed her how quickly it worked, she was very excited.

Mrs Cocoa was so excited that she hurried out into her back-garden, and called to my little sister who was playing in our garden, 'Come and see what Mr Jones has bought for me!' she called, and my little sister ran and fetched her dolly, Rosy-primrose, to see too.

Then my little sister hurried through her very own little gate into Mr Cocoa's garden, then through the backdoor into Mrs Cocoa's shiny-clean kitchen. THEN MY LITTLE SISTER STOPPED. She stood still and *listened*.

There was a funny, humming noise coming from Mrs Cocoa's sitting-room, and my little sister didn't like it.

'Come in,' said Mrs Cocoa, 'come and see my new cleaner.'

Then my little sister walked forward, and looked in at the sitting-room door. She had never seen a vacuum cleaner before, so she stared and stared and listened and listened. And she didn't like it one bit!

'I don't like it!' said my naughty little sister. 'I want to go home!'

Then Mr Cocoa switched off the cleaner and the

noise stopped, but my little sister still didn't like it. 'I want to go home,' she said.

'But it's to help poor Mrs Cocoa do her work,' said Mr Cocoa in his nice kind voice. 'It will eat all the nasty dust for her.'

'*I* help Mrs Cocoa,' said my sister. 'I help Mrs Cocoa do the work!' and she began to cry and cry, and she ran right out of Mrs Cocoa's tidy clean house and back to our house, crying and crying. AND SHE WOULDN'T GO TO SEE MRS COCOA AT ALL.

My little sister would not go into Mrs Cocoa's house for a long while, and, if she heard the cleaner working when she was playing in our garden she ran straight in to our mother and hid her face in our mother's apron, because she didn't like the noise the cleaner made.

Now Mrs Cocoa Jones was very very sad when my little sister wouldn't come to see her, because she loved my bad little sister very much. The vacuum cleaner did a lot of work for Mrs Cocoa, and her bad back was a good deal better, but Mrs Cocoa was still sad. So she spoke to Mr Cocoa, and he said he would have a word with my little sister and see if he could make her like the vacuum after all.

One morning when Mr Cocoa was digging his garden, and my little sister was blowing some of the lovely white fluffy seeds from a dandelion flower, Mr Cocoa said, 'I should think our Charlie would like some of that fluff.'

My little sister was very surprised to hear Mr Cocoa say this because she didn't know anything about Charlie.

'Poor Charlie gets so hungry,' said Mr Cocoa Jones, 'and all we can give him to eat is dust and dirt – and he does love some nice fluff if he can get it.'

'What Charlie?' said my little sister. 'What Charlie is hungry?'

'Charlie the cleaner,' said clever Mr Cocoa. 'Charlie who eats the dirt for Mrs Cocoa. There's not a lot of dirt in our house you know,' he said, 'poor old Charlie.'

Mr Cocoa spoke so nicely that Charlie sounded just like a poor hungry boy and my little sister felt quite sorry about him. So she gave Mr Cocoa the dandelion flower seeds and said, 'For Charlie,' and Mr Cocoa took them indoors.

Then my little sister heard the sound of Mrs Cocoa's cleaner, but this time she didn't run indoors, she stood and listened to the sound poor Charlie made when he ate the dandelion fluff and she was quite glad to think that she had given it to him.

When Mr Cocoa came out again, my little sister said, 'Did Charlie like it?' and Mr Cocoa said, 'Yes, it was a treat for him.' So then my little sister went up and down the garden and picked a lot of dandelion clocks for Charlie.

'Why don't you come and give them to him?' said Mr Cocoa. 'Come and see him eat them all up. Poor old Charlie,' Mr Cocoa said.

'Poor old Charlie,' said my little sister, and because she was quite sorry for poor Charlie, she went into Mrs Cocoa's house to see him.

When my little sister really looked at poor Charlie she wasn't a bit frightened. She saw that he had a round shiny body and a long trunk-thing. There was a shiny handle fixed to Charlie's trunk that had a black mouth-looking thing at the end of it.

'Hello Charlie Cocoa,' said my little sister, 'you are a funny looking boy.'

When Mr Cocoa switched on Charlie's noise, my little sister didn't like it at all, but she wasn't frightened any more. She laughed and put her hands over her ears, and watched as Charlie ate up all the dandelion seeds. He was hungry! My little sister knew that there *wouldn't* be very much for him on Mrs Cocoa's clean floors. She knew that you had to do a great deal of brushing to get even a little dust from those carpets.

My little sister was so sorry for Charlie, that, can you ever guess what she did? She went to Mrs Cocoa's broom cupboard, and got out her own little dustpan and brush, and then she went out into Mrs Cocoa's garden, and swept up a nice pan of dust from the path, and brought it in and gave it to him.

'There, Charlie, eat it up do,' my little sister said. 'Poor Charlie! Poor Charlie Cocoa!'

17

My Naughty Little Sister and
the Book Little Boy

Do you like having stories read to you? When I was a little girl I used to like it very much. My little sister liked it too, but she pretended that she didn't.

When my sister and I were very little children we had a kind aunt who used to come and read stories to us. She used to read all the stories that she'd had read to her when *she* was a little girl.

I used to listen and listen and say, 'Go on! Go on!' whenever my auntie stopped for a minute, but my little sister used to pretend that she wasn't listening. Wasn't she silly? She used to fidget with her old doll, Rosy-primrose, and pretend that she was playing babies with her, but really she listened and listened too, and *heard every word*.

Do you know how I knew that she listened and listened? I'll tell you. When my little sister was in bed at night she used to tell the stories all over again to Rosy-primrose.

One day when my aunt came to read to us, she said, 'I've got a book here that I won as a Sunday

School prize. I used to like these stories when I was a child, I hope you will like them too.'

So our aunt read us a story about a poor little boy. It was a very sad story in the beginning because this poor little boy was very ragged and hungry. It

said that he had no breakfast and no dinner and no supper, but it was lovely at the end because a nice kind lady took him home with her and said she was his real mother and gave him lots of nice things to eat and lots of nice clothes to wear, and a white pony. But the 'nothing to eat' part was very sad.

Now, you know, my little sister liked eating, and she was so surprised to hear about the book little boy with nothing to eat that she forgot to pretend that she wasn't listening and she said, 'No break-fast?' She said 'no breakfast' in a very little voice.

Our auntie said, 'No, no breakfast.'

My little sister said, 'No dinner?' She said that in a little voice too, because she thought no dinner and no breakfast was terrible.

My aunt said, 'No dinner, *and* no supper,' and she was so pleased to think that my funny little sister *had* been listening that she said, 'Would you like to see the picture?' And my little sister said 'please' and I said 'please' too.

So our kind aunt showed us the picture in the book that went with the poor little boy story. It was a very miserable picture because the little boy was sitting all alone in the corner of a room, looking very sad. There was an empty plate on the floor beside this poor little boy, and under the picture it said, '*Nothing to eat.*'

Wasn't that sad?

My little sister thought it was very sad. She looked and looked at the picture and she said, '*No* breakfast, NO dinner, and NO SUPPER.' Like that, over and over again.

My aunt said, 'Cheer up. He had lots to eat when his kind rich mother took him home in the end, he had a pony too, remember,' my aunt said.

But my sister said, 'No *picture* dinner. Poor, poor boy,' she said.

Well now, when the reading time was over my little sister was a very quiet child. She was very quiet when she had her supper. She sat by the fire and my mother gave her a big piece of buttery bread and a big mug of warm sweet milk, but she was very quiet, she said 'thank you' in a tiny quiet voice, and she drank up her milk like a good child. When my mother came to say that the hot-water bottle was in her bed, she said her prayers in a good quiet way and went straight upstairs.

My mother kissed my warm little sister and said 'good night' to her, and my little sister said 'good night.' But when my kind aunt kissed her and said 'good night' to her, my little sister said, '*No* breakfast, NO dinner,' and my auntie said, 'No supper,' but my little sister smiled and said, 'YES, SUPPER.' My little sister looked very smily and pleased with herself.

Wasn't that a funny thing to say, '*No* breakfast, NO dinner and YES, SUPPER'? My aunt thought it was funny, and so did my mother. They said, 'What a funny child you are.'

But when our aunt went to go home, and looked for the Sunday School prize-book, she knew why my little sister had said such a funny thing.

Do you know what that silly child had done? She had put her piece of buttery bread inside the Sunday School prize-book, on top of the little book boy's picture. She had given her supper to the book little boy!

Of course the book was very greasy and crumby after that, which was a pity because our aunt had kept it very tidy indeed as it had been a prize. I suppose it was a very naughty thing to have done.

But my little sister hadn't *meant* to be naughty. She thought that she had given the book little boy her own supper, and you know she was quite a greedy child, so it was a kind thing to do really.

Now you know why she said, '*No* breakfast, NO dinner, and YES, SUPPER,' don't you?

18

Bad Harry's Haircut

QUITE a long time ago, when I was a little girl, my Naughty Little Sister used to play with a little boy called Harry.

This boy Harry only lived a little way away from us, and as there were no nasty roads to cross between our houses, Harry used to come all on his own to play with my little sister, and she used to go all on her own to play with him. And they were Very Good Friends.

AND they were both very NAUGHTY CHILDREN. Oh dear!

But, if you could have seen this Bad Harry you wouldn't have said that he was a naughty child. He looked so very good. Yes, he looked very good indeed.

My little sister never looked very good, even when she was behaving herself, but Bad Harry looked good all the time.

My naughty little sister's friend Harry had big, big blue eyes and pretty golden curls like a baby angel, but oh dear, he was quite naughty all the same.

Now one day, when my little sister went round to play with Harry she found him looking very smart indeed. He was wearing real big boy's trousers. Real ones, with real big boy's buttons and real big boy's braces! Red braces like a very big boy! Wasn't he smart?

'Look,' said Bad Harry, 'Look at my big boys' trousers.'

'Smart,' said my naughty little sister, 'smart boy.'

'I'm going to have a real boy's haircut too,' said Bad Harry. 'Today. Not Mummy with scissors any more; but a real boy's haircut in a real barber's shop!'

My word, he was a proud boy!

My little sister was *so* surprised, and Bad Harry was *so* pleased to see how surprised she was.

'I'll be a big boy then,' he said.

Then Harry's mother, who was a kind lady and liked my little sister very much, said that if she was a good girl she could come to the barber's and see Harry have his haircut.

My little sister was so excited that she ran straight back home at once to tell our mother all about Harry's big boy's trousers and Harry's real boy's haircut. 'Can I go too, can I go too?' she asked our mother.

Our mother said, 'Yes, you may go, only hold very

tight to Harry's mother's hand when you cross the High Street,' and my little sister promised that she would hold very tight indeed.

So off they went to the barber's to get Harry a Real Boy's Haircut.

My little sister had never been in a barber's shop before and she stared and stared. Bad Harry had never been in a barber's shop before either, but he didn't stare, he pretended that he knew all about it, he picked up one of the barber's books and pretended to look at the pictures in it, but he peeped all the time at the barber's shop.

There were three haircut-men in the barber's shop, and they all had white coats and they all had black combs sticking out of their pockets.

There were three white wash-basins with shiny taps and looking-glasses, and three very funny chairs. In the three funny chairs were three men all having something done to them by the three haircut-men.

One man was having his hair cut with scissors, and one man was having his neck clipped with clippers, and one man had a soapy white face and *he* was being shaved!

And there were bottles and bottles, and brushes and brushes, and towels and towels, and pretty pictures with writing on them, and all sorts of things to see! My little sister looked and Bad Harry peeped until it was Harry's turn to have his hair cut.

When it was Harry's turn one of the haircut-men fetched a special high-chair for Harry to sit in, because the grown-up chairs were all too big.

Harry sat in the special chair and then the haircut-man got a big blue sheet and wrapped it round Harry and tucked it in at the neck. 'You don't want any tickly old hairs going down there,' the haircut-man said.

Then the haircut-man took his sharp shiny scissors and began to cut and cut. And, *down* fell a golden curl and 'Gone!' said my little sister, and down fell another golden curl and 'Gone!' said my little sister again, and she said 'Gone!' 'Gone!' 'Gone!' all the time until Harry's curls had quite gone away. Then she said, 'All gone now!'

When the haircut-man had finished cutting, he took a bottle with a squeezer-thing and he squirted some nice smelly stuff all over Harry's head, and made Harry laugh, and my little sister laughed as well.

Then the haircut-man took the big black comb, and he made a Big Boy's Parting on Harry's head, and he combed Harry's hair back into a real boy's haircut and then Bad Harry climbed down from the high-chair so that my little sister could really look at him.

And then my little sister *did* stare. Bad Harry's mother stared too. . . .

For there was that bad boy Harry, with his real boy's trousers and his real boy's braces, with a REAL BOY'S HAIRCUT, smiling and smiling, and looking very pleased.

'No curls now,' said Bad Harry. 'Not any more.'

'No curls,' said my naughty little sister.

'No,' Bad Harry's mother said, 'and oh dear! you don't even *look* good any more.'

Then my little sister laughed and laughed. 'Bad Harry!' she said. 'Bad Harry. All bad now – like me!'

19

My Naughty Little Sister
wins a Prize

A LONG time ago, when I was a little girl, my naughty little sister, who was smaller than me, had a lot of friends, but her favourite friends were the nice coalman, and the nice milkman, and the baker with a poor bad leg, and the window-cleaner man, and her very, very favourite friend was called Mr Blakey and he had a shoe-mending shop, and had rather a cross and roary voice.

Now one day everyone where we lived became very excited, because they heard that the town was going to have a GRAND CARNIVAL.

Everyone talked and talked about the Carnival because the town had never had a Carnival before, and there were pictures of funny clowns with writing underneath in all the shop windows and stuck up on all the fences. The clown was to show how jolly and funny the Grand Carnival was going to be, and the writing was to tell about all the nice things that would be happening when Carnival Day came.

My little sister liked the clown-picture very much, and because she wasn't old enough to read, she asked our mother to tell her what the writing was about, and she asked QUESTIONS and QUESTIONS.

My mother told her that all the shops would be shut and there would be swings and roundabouts in the park, and a band.

My little sister asked more QUESTIONS and QUESTIONS, and my father told her that there would be pony-rides and toe-dancing and fireworks and a flower-show.

But my little sister still asked questions and questions until at last our father and mother said, 'You must wait and see for yourself when Carnival Day comes.'

Well now, there was one thing about the Grand Carnival that my little sister liked to hear best of all, and that was the GRAND PROCESSION AND FANCY DRESS PARADE.

Do you know what that means? It means that lots of people dress up in beautiful clothes or funny clothes and they go through all the streets of the town so that everyone can see them. Some of the people walk, and some ride in cars or on lorries or bicycles, and the people who look the most beautiful or the funniest, win prizes.

Do you know why my little sister was so interested in the Grand Procession and Fancy Dress Parade? It was because all her special friends were going to be in it.

When the nice coalman came, he told my naughty little sister that he was going to wash down the coal-cart and put lovely red ribbons on his horse, and that all the Infant School children were going to ride with him. He said that the Infant School children were going to be dressed up as fairies and pixies. The nice coalman said that *he* wasn't going to be a fairy or a pixie, but that he was going to wear his Sunday-best hat, so, of course, my little sister wanted to see him very much.

The nice milkman said he was going to have lots of flags on his cart, and that all the pretty ladies from the dairy shop were going to be dressed up to look like milkmaids, and walk beside it with milking pails. The milkman said that he was going to be dressed up, too.

When my little sister asked the milkman what he was going to be dressed up *as*, the milkman said, 'Ah! Just you wait and see! I'll be very fancy, I promise you!'

That sounded so exciting that my little sister wanted to see *him* very much indeed.

The nice baker said that he was going to leave his cart at home because he was going to march *with his medals up* with the other old soldiers. That did sound grand – 'march with his medals up.'

My little sister could hardly wait to see the nice baker marching with his poor bad leg along with all the other old soldiers, and she told the nice baker that she would keep a very special look-out for *him*.

When the window-cleaner man came, he said that he was going to dress his barrow up with roses and roses, and that his little niece was going to be a rose-fairy on the top. Didn't that sound pretty? My little sister thought it did, and she said, 'I wish the Grand Carnival Day would HURRY UP!'

My little sister was so pleased and so excited about the Carnival that she went in to see her dear friend Mr Blakey at the shoe-mending shop to see what *he* was going to dress up as.

But Mr Blakey said he was too old for dressing up and being a poppy-show. He said that if everyone dressed up and walked in the Grand Procession there wouldn't be anyone to watch it, and then there would be no reason for dressing-up at all. Mr Blakey said he was going to be a SPECTATOR.

My naughty little sister did not know what 'spectator' meant so Mr Blakey said it meant *some-one who looked on*.

So my little sister said, 'I will be a Spectator too, and Mother will be a Spectator, and Father will be a Spectator, and my big sister will be a Spectator.' And she was very pleased indeed.

BUT my naughty little sister wasn't a spectator. NO she was *something else*.

This is what happened:

The day before the Grand Carnival Day, the window-cleaner man came to our house. He didn't bring his barrow, he came on a bicycle and looked very worried.

The window-cleaner man told my mother that his little niece was not a well girl, and that she had got to stay in bed for a few days. He said she wouldn't be able to be the rose-fairy on his barrow after all, and he asked my mother if she would let my little sister ride on his barrow instead. He said that my little sister was just the same size as his little niece, so that the rose-fairy frock would fit her nicely.

Wasn't that a lovely idea? It was very sad about the poor little not-well niece wasn't it? But it was lovely for my naughty little sister.

My little sister said, 'Please let me, please. PLEASE do.'

My mother said, 'I don't know. You do get into such dreadful mischief.'

But the window-cleaner man said, 'She can't come to any harm on the barrow.'

And my little sister said, 'I will be good – I will be very very good. I PROMISE.'

So at last my mother said, 'Well, if it's a fine day tomorrow, she may go.'

The window-cleaner man and my little sister were both very pleased when our mother said this, and they were more pleased still next morning, when they saw the bright sunshine, and knew that it was going to be a fine day.

So, my little sister was dressed up in the beautiful rose-fairy dress that the poor little ill niece had been going to wear, and it was a *perfect fit*.

The rose-fairy dress was pink, and *sticking out*, and it had dear little green wings – just like leaves.

When my little sister was dressed she ran through her own little gate in the back-garden to see Mr and Mrs Cocoa Jones who lived next door, to show them how smart she was, and Mrs Cocoa said that she looked just like a real fairy.

My naughty little sister was so pleased that she danced a special little made-up dance for them. She would have danced for a long time, only my mother called, 'Hurry up, or the Parade will start without you.'

So my little sister went off with my mother through the town to the place that the procession was to start from, and everyone stared as they went by, to see such a very pretty rose-fairy in the street, and my little sister held tight to Mother's hand and looked very pleased and smily. She was a proud girl!

She was prouder still when she saw the window-cleaning barrow, because it looked so beautiful. It was covered with so many beautiful roses that you couldn't see that it was a barrow at all, and there was a dear little chair made of roses for my little sister to sit on, and a sunshade of rose-petals for her to hold.

(They weren't real roses, of course – they were made of paper, but they looked *very* real. I thought you would be wondering about the prickles if I didn't explain this.)

The window-cleaner man had a smart white coat on, and a new straw hat, with a rose in his button-hole, and he was very glad to see how pretty my little sister looked. 'You are a credit to your family,' he said to her, and he lifted her up very carefully into the little chair, and our mother spread out her sticking-out skirt, and tidied her wings and made her look really lovely.

While she was waiting for the parade to start, she looked at all the other fancy-dressed people, and they were all very lovely too. She saw her friend the coalman with his cart. He looked very clean and nice – not a bit coaly today, and his cart had lots of tree-branches tied all over it, and all the Infant School children were in the cart, laughing and shouting, and waving their fairy wands. The coal-man didn't see my little sister, because he was walking along beside the horse, but she saw him and his Sunday best hat, too.

My little sister saw her friend the milkman as well, although he looked so funny that she hardly knew him, but she knew his cart, and she knew the young ladies from the shop – even though they were all dressed up as milkmaids! The milkman had a tall black hat like a chimney-pot, and his nose was painted red, and he looked a little bit like the clown on the GRAND CARNIVAL pictures. The milkman saw my little sister and he waved to her. But my little sister didn't wave back, she sat still and quiet, because she wanted to be good today.

She didn't see the baker because all the Old Soldiers were walking at the front of the parade, behind the band, but she saw lots of other old soldiers with their medals up, and they all looked so smart and nice, and their medals were so shiny, that she knew the poor bad-leg baker must be looking very grand indeed.

Then the band began to play, and the procession

started. The window-cleaner man said 'Ups-adaisy,' and he took up the handles of his barrow – that you couldn't see for roses and roses – and off they went, and everyone saw my pretty little rose-fairy sister, with her dress spread out nicely, and her leafy little wings sticking up quite straight – looking as good as gold.

Mr Blakey hadn't known that my little sister was going to be in the procession, and he *was* surprised when he saw her going by. He waved and waved, and said, 'Bravo-hooray,' until my little sister saw him. When she did, she waved to him and blew him a little kiss, and then she sat good and still again, while the window-cleaner man pushed and pushed.

And what do you think? When the Grand Procession and Fancy Dress Parade was over, the window-cleaner man got a first prize for his beautiful rose barrow. AND my little sister was given a special prize for looking so beautiful and being so good.

The window-cleaner man had a little wooden clock for his prize, and my little sister had a baby doll with shutting eyes and a long white dress.

The window-cleaner man said that my little sister had been a thoroughly good child, and when my little sister thanked him for taking her, he said it was a treat to have her with him.

Then she did a kind and generous thing, she did it all her own self, without anyone telling her to.

My little sister remembered that poor ill little niece who couldn't wear the nice dress or go in the parade – so she gave the shutting-eye doll to the window-cleaner man and asked him to give it to his poor ill niece, who couldn't be in the procession. Wasn't that nice of her?

My little sister said she was very, very sorry about the ill little niece, but that she was very glad all the same to have been in the Grand Procession.

The window-cleaner man said that next time there was a Carnival, he would put two little chairs on his barrow, and then my little sister and his little niece could be fairies together.

20

My Naughty Little Sister
and the Workmen

WHEN my sister was a naughty little girl, she was a very, very inquisitive child. She was always looking and peeping into things that didn't belong to her. She used to open other people's cupboards and boxes just to find out what was inside.

Aren't you glad you aren't inquisitive like that?

Well now, one day a lot of workmen came to dig up all the roads near our house, and my little sister was very interested in them. They were very nice men, but some of them had rather loud shouty voices sometimes. There were shovelling men, and picking men, and men with jumping-about things that went, 'Ah-ah-ah-ah-ah-ah-aha-aaa,' and men who drank tea out of jam-pots, and men who cooked sausages over fires, and there was an old, old man who sat up all night when the other men had gone home, and who had a lot of coats and scarves to keep him warm.

There were lots of things for my little inquisitive sister to see, there were heaps of earth, and red lanterns for the old, old man to light at night-time, and long pole-y things to keep people from falling down the holes in the road, and workmen's huts, and many other things.

When the workmen were in our road, my little sister used to watch them every day. She used to lean over the gate and stare and stare, but when they went off to the next road she didn't see so much of them.

Well now, I will tell you about the inquisitive thing my naughty little sister did one day, shall I?

Yes. Well, do you remember Bad Harry who was my little sister's best boy-friend? Do you? I thought you did. Now this Bad Harry came one day to ask my mother if my little sister could go round to his house to play with him, and as Bad Harry's house wasn't far away, and as there were no roads to cross, my mother said my little sister could go.

So my little sister put on her hat and her coat, and her scarf and her gloves, because it was a cold nasty day, and went off with her best boy-friend to play with him.

They hurried along like good children until they came to the workmen in the next road, and then they went slow as slow, because there were so many things to see. They looked at this, and at that, and when they got past the workmen they found a very curious thing.

By the road there was a tall hedge, and under the tall hedge there was a mackintoshy bundle.

Now this mackintoshy bundle hadn't anything to do with Bad Harry, and it hadn't anything to do with my naughty little sister, yet, do you know, they were so inquisitive that they stopped and looked at it.

They had such a good look at it that they had to get right under the hedge to see, and when they got very near it they found it was an old mackintosh wrapped round something or other inside.

Weren't they naughty? They should have gone straight home to Bad Harry's mother's house, shouldn't they? But they didn't. They stayed and looked at the mackintoshy bundle.

And they opened it. They really truly did. It wasn't their bundle, but they opened it wide under the hedge, and do you know what was inside it? I know you aren't an inquisitive meddlesome child, but would you like to know?

Well, inside the bundle there were lots and lots of parcels and packages tied up in red handkerchiefs, and brown paper, and newspaper, and instead of putting them back again like nice children, those little horrors started to open all those parcels, and inside those parcels there were lots of things to eat!

There were sandwiches, and cakes and meat pies and cold cooked fish, and eggs, and goodness knows what-all.

Weren't those bad children surprised? They couldn't think how all those sandwiches and things could have got into that old mackintosh.

Then Bad Harry said, 'Shall we eat some?' You remember he was a greedy lad. But my little sister said, 'No, it's picked-up food.' My little sister knew that my mother had told her never never, to eat picked-up food. You see she was good about *that*.

Only she was very bad after, because she said, 'I know, let's play with it.'

So they took out all those sandwiches and cakes, and meat-pies and cold cooked fish and eggs, and they laid them out across the path and made them into pretty patterns on the ground. Then Bad Harry threw a sandwich at my little sister and she threw a meat-pie at him, and they began to have a lovely game.

And then, do you know what happened? A big

roary voice called out, 'WHAT ARE YOU DOING WITH OUR DINNERS, YOU MONKEYS – YOU?' And there was a big workman coming towards them, looking so cross and angry that those two bad children screamed and screamed, and because the workman was so roary they turned and ran and ran back down the road, and the big workman ran after them as cross as cross. Weren't they frightened?

When they got back to where the other roadmen were digging, those children were more frightened than ever, because the big workman shouted to all the other workmen about what those naughty children had done with their dinners.

Yes, those poor workmen had put all their dinners under the hedge in the old mackintosh to keep them dry and safe until dinner-time. As well as being frightened, Bad Harry and my naughty little sister were very ashamed.

They were so ashamed that they did a most silly thing. When they heard the big workman telling the others about their dinners, those silly children ran and hid themselves in one of the pipes that the workmen were putting in the road.

My naughty little sister went first, and old Bad Harry after her. Because my naughty little sister was so frightened she wriggled in and in the pipe, and Bad Harry came wriggling after her, because he was frightened too.

And then a dreadful thing happened to my naughty little sister. That Bad Harry *stuck in the pipe* – and he couldn't get any farther. He was quite a round fat boy, you see, and he stuck fast as fast in the pipe.

Then didn't those sillies howl and howl.

My little sister howled because she didn't want to go on and on down the roadmen's pipes on her own, and Bad Harry howled because he couldn't move at all.

It was all terrible of course, but the roary workman rescued them very quickly. He couldn't reach Bad Harry with his arm, but he got a long hooky iron thing, and he hooked it in Bad Harry's belt, and he pulled and pulled, and presently he pulled Bad Harry out of the pipe. Wasn't it a good thing they had the hooky iron? And wasn't it a *very* good thing that Bad Harry had a strong belt on his coat?

When Bad Harry was out, my little sister wriggled back and back, and came out too, and when she saw all the poor workmen who wouldn't have any dinner, she cried and cried, and she told them what a sorry girl she was. She told the workmen that she and Bad Harry hadn't known the mackintoshy bundle was their dinners, and Bad Harry said he was sorry too, and they were so really truly ashamed that the big workman said, 'Well, never mind this time. It's pay-day today, so we can send the boy for fish and chips instead,' and he told my little sister not to cry any more.

So my little sister stopped crying, and she and Bad Harry both said they would never, never meddle and be inquisitive again.

There now, what do you think about all the stories about my naughty little sister? Don't you think she is a bad child, and aren't you glad you are not like that?

Twelve of *My Naughty Little Sister* stories have been recorded by Delysé Records. They are read by Kaye Webb and distributed by Decca. (DEL 198 to 205.)

SOME OTHER YOUNG PUFFINS
WHICH YOU MIGHT ENJOY

The Happy Orpheline *Natalie Savage Carlson*

The twenty little orphaned girls who live with Madame Flattot are terrified of being adopted because they are so happy.

Five Dolls in a House *Helen Clare*

A little girl called Elizabeth finds a way of making herself small and visits her dolls in their own house.

Three Little Funny Ones *Charlotte Hough*

Oliver, Timmy and Tom have some adventures which are just frightening enough to make them interesting, like when they make a lion trap and catch a sausage dog. (Also available in Initial Teaching Alphabet.)

Meet Mary Kate *Helen Morgan*

Charmingly told stories of a four-year-old's everyday life in the country. Illustrated by Shirley Hughes.

Little Old Mrs Pepperpot *Alf Prøysen*
Mrs Pepperpot to the Rescue

Gay little stories about an old woman who suddenly shrinks to the size of a pepperpot.

Dear Teddy Robinson *Joan G. Robinson*

Teddy Robinson was Deborah's teddy bear and such a very nice, friendly cuddly bear that he went everywhere with her and had even more adventures than she did.

The Adventures of Galldora *Modwena Sedgwick*

This lovable rag doll belonged to Marybell, who wasn't always very careful to look after her, so Galldora was always getting lost – in a field with a scarecrow, on top of a roof, and in all sorts of other strange places.

Clever Polly and the Stupid Wolf *Catherine Storr*

Clever Polly manages to think of lots of good ideas to stop the stupid wolf from eating her.

Robin *Catherine Storr*

Robin was the youngest of three, and hated it. And then he discovered the shell called the Freedom of the Seas – and became the wonder of his family.

Danny Fox *David Thomson*

Clever Danny Fox helps the Princess to marry the fisherman she loves and comes safely home to his hungry family. (*A Young Puffin Original*.)

Danny Fox Meets a Stranger *David Thomson*

The stranger was a big grey wolf, and he was out to steal Danny's den and hunting grounds. (*A Young Puffin Original*.)

The Urchin *Edith Unnerstad*

The Urchin is only five years old – but already he has the Larsson family at sixes and sevens with his ingenious tricks and adventures.

Little O *Edith Unnerstad*

The enchanting story of the youngest of the Pip Larsson family.

Magic in My Pocket *Alison Uttley*

A selection of short stories by this well-loved author, especially good for 5- and 6-year olds.